My Sexy Veterinarian

Bonnie Phelps

Lilac Lace Press

Learn more about Bonnie and her books at her website:
www.bonniephelpsauthor.com

Have a question or comment? Send Bonnie an email at:
bonnie@bonniephelpsauthor.com

ISBN: 13: 978-0-9989303-1-2
ISBN- 10: 0-9989303-1-8

DEDICATION

To my amazing husband for all of his support and for introducing me to the meaning of true romance! To my daughters for all their encouragement and support.

ACKNOWLEDGMENTS

Thank you to my critique partners – Elsa Bayly and Pegi Palmes – for reading multiple first drafts and helping fine tune my manuscript. I take each and every suggestion to heart. Thank you also to my fellow Romance Writers of America friends and colleagues, especially my Yosemite Romance Writer and Sacramento Valley Rose Chapter mates. Your friendship and well-aimed head slaps makes each book I write better. A special thank you to my editor, Anna J. Stewart. You rock! Your guidance helped take my writing to new heights.

CONTENTS

CONTENTS

CHAPTER ONE

Heat from the grill hit Nate Kincaid like a blast furnace. He had to wonder whose bright idea it was to make Labor Day—when temperatures routinely climbed into the high 90's to low 100's in the Texas Hill Country—a day for barbecuing. The tantalizing aroma of the ribs he basted with his family's secret sauce *almost* made up for the heat. He swiped a bandana across his forehead and back of his neck, then shoved it in a pocket of his swim trunks.

Glancing up at the clear, blue sky, he admired the fingers of white clouds stretching across the horizon. He appreciated the contrast between the manicured backyard of his parent's ranch compound and the rugged pastures and the gray outlines of the distant hills beyond. The sound of children cannonballing into the pool drew his attention and a smile as those seated within striking distance shrieked at the inevitable dousing they got.

Lifting the lid on a second grill, he used the tongs to turn the corn on the cob, transferring the done ones to a nearby platter. His stomach rumbled as the earthy scent of the charred husks filled his nostrils. His taste buds eager for the first taste of the sweet kernels dripping with butter and dusted with salt.

Must be about time for someone to relieve him so he could eat and mingle. He'd especially like to mingle with the cute brunette by the pool. He'd dated her once, or was that twice? He shrugged. No matter. She was fun and didn't expect professions of undying love, but if he didn't get over there soon, one of his cousins was sure to swoop in. Then he'd either have to battle for her attention—possibly leading his mom to incorrect assumptions and false hope—or he'd have to target one of the other lovely single ladies in attendance. He swept the area like a hawk searching for prey. Option two would work just fine.

Contentment filled Nate like air in a balloon, expanding and light. Yup, life as it should be. Surrounded by family and friends. Plenty of food to fill hungry bellies. Laughter, friendly gossip, casual flirting, the women tending the little ones, and the men tending grills and talking sports. Everything in its place. Exactly the way he liked it.

The sight of his mom, Gloria June, marching at him like a battalion of determined soldiers, his youngest brother in tow, made his shoulders sag and resignation sink into him like syrup on a pancake, sticky and thick. He was reminded peace and contentment could flee in the blink of an eye into the nearest dark cave like bats at dawn. That sweet smile on her face didn't fool him one bit. The fire in her eyes signaled loud and clear she'd talked to Jennifer's mom and discovered he'd side-stepped her latest attempt to hog tie him to what she hoped would be the woman of his dreams. A burning sensation lodged at the top of his stomach, dissolving the quiet order of his life.

Why couldn't his family butt out and let him be? He was fine. His life was fine. Why did everyone want to fix what wasn't broken. Didn't he have enough to deal with building his business and paying off the debt on his place? Couldn't they see that's where his focus needed to be right now?

His lips curved up in what he hoped was a disarming smile. "Hi Mom. Just in time. I've got ribs, burgers, and corn on the cob ready to go. Want to take this platter over to the food table?"

"In a minute. Brought Josh over to take his turn at the grill and give you a break." She tugged her youngest son forward and slapped the barbecue tongs into his waiting hand. Wrapping an arm around Nate's arm, she gave him little choice but to fall in step beside her.

2

He narrowed his eyes and tilted his head down so he could look into her face. Not liking what he saw, he dug his flip flop clad feet into the ground and refused to budge his 6'5" frame. "Where, exactly, are you leading me?"

"You haven't eaten yet and Jennifer is *sitting all by herself.*" She waved at the pretty young woman sitting at one of the tables set out on the lawn. The lady in question waggled her fingers in return, hope in her face. "I thought you could keep each other company."

He swallowed past the lump in his throat. Deliberately disappointing another person twisted his insides like a pickle jar lid and left the same sour taste.

If he was getting out of this, he had to start tap dancing— and fast. Defer. Deflect. Divert. He hated when people pushed him. He would decide when, where, and with who he would do things.

"You're right, Mom. Jennifer is a great girl." He crossed his arms against his chest and angled his head. He paused a beat, like he was thinking. "But don't you think she's more Zach's type? Comes from a rodeo family and is much closer to his age than mine. Strikes me as someone who'd be happy following him around the country. Adventurous. I don't have much in common with her."

"Doing your brother a favor, are you?" She eyed him like he was as transparent as a jelly fish.

"Exactly." His middle brother was a master at casual relationships. The tiny prickle of guilt he felt at passing this problem along to Zach, hardly registered on his personal Richter scale. "I think you should go find Zach right now and introduce him to Jennifer." He cupped her shoulders and rotated her in the general direction of the party. His brother was sure to be in the thick of the action, or out behind the barn with his latest conquest.

He felt his mother's resistance and prepared himself for the assault.

Gloria June turned to face him, hands on hips. "Nathaniel David Kincaid. *Do not* try and bamboozle me. I know all your

3

tricks." She paused and a thoughtful expression crossed her face. His stomach felt like someone had attached lead weights and tossed it into the lake. She was going to fight him on this. He wasn't about to get serious about Jennifer just to make his mom happy. She wasn't—his mind closed like a steel trap. No, he wasn't going there.

His mother patted his cheek. "I'll let you off the hook—this time. She probably is a better match for Zach."

He couldn't stop the grin spreading across his face. Dodged one this time.

A finger flicked like a pendulum in front of his face. "But I'm not giving up on you." She took a deep breath and gently grasped his arm. "Son, we worry about you. It's time you found a way to move on. Sharon's gone. Nothing can bring her back."

The sucker punch of fear and pain sliced through his gut, anger close on its heels as heat flushed up his neck. He knew the anger he directed at his mom was irrational. She wanted him to be happy, but people needed to stop pushing him.

"Mom, I *am* moving on with my life. I'm building my career. I'll find the right woman eventually, but Not. Right. Now." It was time people stopped treating him like a kid. He knew what was best for him.

"Honey, we appreciate how responsible you are, but don't you see, you're marking time, not living." A sly smile crossed her face. He braced for her next words. "Besides, it's about time you settled down and started a family. You're not getting any younger and I want more grandbabies." She patted his arm. "I'll go find your brother and practice my match-making skills on him."

Nate watched her stride away. His heart rate slowed with each step she took. Finally he was able to draw a deep breath and fill his lungs. He closed his eyes and massaged his throbbing temples with his fingertips. What did a man have to do to get his family off his back?

A steady girlfriend would do it. He didn't want one of those. What he needed was someone he could pass off as a serious love interest. Someone believable, who wouldn't set off his mom's BS meter. Someone who wouldn't expect more than he could give. Surely there was a woman like that out there somewhere.

****

Lauren Royall unfolded her 5'10" body from Crystal Kincaid's Jeep Cherokee and stretched her arms over her head, bending from side to side to work out the kinks. They'd arrived at the Rocking K Ranch, about 45 minutes outside town for the Kincaid family's annual Labor Day barbecue. She closed her eyes and assumed a Namaste pose, palms together in front of her chest. Serene. Confident. Slowly becoming one with the sounds and smells around her. People might look askance, but she didn't care.

The bright sun warmed her. Sweet alyssum must be somewhere nearby, its spicy smell drifting by on the light breeze, mingling with what? She inhaled deeply. The aroma of meat on the grill floated by, faint but inviting. Even though she didn't eat a lot of red meat, she was willing to indulge when the urge struck. She wasn't about to let herself be defined by any one lifestyle choice, happy to mix and match as whim led her. Her friends knew she was unpredictable and loved her for it.

She opened her eyes. Hands on hips, stance like a conquering general, she surveyed the scene. A hacienda-style home spread out in front of her. The sweet alyssum she'd smelled trailed along the veranda backed by the bold colors of geraniums, Mexican sage, purple corn flowers, and bright yellow marigolds. A large vegetable garden dominated an area on the far side of the house. Several barns sat nearby. Huge oaks unfurled their massive limbs in an adjacent pasture. Children jostled for their turn on the tire swings suspended from the trees. Quintessential Americana.

Lauren grinned at her friend. "Thanks for inviting me. Can't wait to experience my first authentic Texas barbecue."

She executed a quick two-step hop that made Crystal laugh.

"If you're expecting cowboys with chaps and spurs and a cow roasting on a spit, you'll be disappointed. Our annual Labor Day event looks a lot like ones you'd see anywhere in the country—*just bigger.*" She hooked her arm through Lauren's and led the way to the backyard. "I'm glad you changed your mind and decided to come."

Once they rounded the corner of the house the noise level increased substantially and a sea of humanity flowed across several acres of lawn. Lauren stopped. Her mouth dropped open and it felt like her brows got stuck in her hairline. "*Big* is an understatement. There must be a couple hundred people here."

Crystal grimaced. "Probably closer to 300—and more are out by the corrals doing cowboy stuff." She sighed and shrugged. "The four Kincaid brothers who settled here in the late 1880s had large families. Multiply that by several generations and…" Her hands swept out in front of her. "Voila. You get this."

"Lead the way," Lauren said. They'd only taken a few steps when she placed a hand on Crystal's arm to stop her. "Who's that big, tall, handsome guy flipping burgers?"

"You mean the one closest to us?"

Lauren looked heavenward. "Do you really think I'd be asking about one of the older guys or the teenagers?" Droll rolled off her tongue smooth as silk. "Yes, I mean the one who looks like Thor."

A prickle of excitement skittered up Lauren's spine at the thought of tangling between the sheets with that hulk of a man. Her reaction surprised her. She'd never felt an instant attraction to a man before. Intuition? She'd followed it before and it hadn't failed her. Yet.

"Okay, stupid question. That fine male specimen is my oldest cousin, Nate. Come on, I'll introduce you. He's currently unattached." They'd only taken a couple more steps when Crystal halted. "Uh, oh. He's being corralled by my Aunt Gloria June—his mom." She glanced at Lauren and cringed. "I think introductions will have to wait."

"Tell me about him." Unattached? Crystal led with that? There was a story here. Lauren could feel it.

Crystal inclined her head toward two chairs under a nearby tree. "Follow me."

Lauren eased herself down onto one of the Adirondack chairs, stretched her long legs in front of her, and loosely curled her fingers around the end of the chair arm. "Okay, I'm listening."

"Bear in mind that because Nate is the oldest of the cousins, he was always put in charge so childhood grudges could cloud my assessment."

"I'll do my best to read between the lines." Lauren laughed and laced her fingers in her lap as though she were interviewing a client. "I'm a psychologist. That's what I'm trained to do."

"He was like a bossy, Mr.-Know-It-All." Crystal rolled her eyes. "Think conscience police. For him guilt was like peanut butter—the thicker you spread it, the better. And when boys started sniffing around his female cousins..." Crystal's hands formed claws. "Grrr. He was beyond annoying."

Memories of her own brothers interrogating her dates brought a soft smile to Lauren's lips. "Ah, the challenge of big brothers. I hear you, girl. It was their mission in life to make mine miserable." She idly twisted a strand of hair around her finger. "What else can you tell me?"

"You can't ever tell him I said this because I'll deny it." Crystal leaned in and whispered. "He's one of the good guys. Loyal, trustworthy, responsible to a fault..."

"Boring. You make him sound like a German Shepard."

Crystal started to laugh. "To someone like you, I guess he does sound dull."

"Someone like me? What's that supposed to mean?" Lauren figured she knew, but wanted to hear her friend say it.

"He's very conventional. You, not so much."

Lauren grinned. "I don't knock conventional. It's a choice. What else?" Lots of guys in this part of the country could be described that way. Why did Crystal think she and Nate wouldn't get along? Lauren might be a teensy bit daring, and she might have a touch of wanderlust, but it wasn't like she went cliff diving.

"He's a veterinarian and formed his own group. Most of his time and energy over the past few years has been focused on building up the clinic's client list. When he lets go, he can be charming and funny—though that's been in short supply since…" Crystal paused, sighed, and her face melted into sadness.

"Since?" Lauren scooted to the edge of her chair and instinctively placed a comforting hand on her friend's arm. Obviously there was some kind of heartbreak in his background. She'd seen it often enough in her practice.

"He was engaged and his fiancé died a few months before the wedding. He's never quite made it back to his old self."

"Maybe he just needs more time." Lauren's heart ached for his loss. So young. Then that warm familiar glow filled her chest. She could help.

"It's been eighteen months since Sharon died. Isn't that enough time?" Crystal asked.

"None of us are ever the same after losing someone so important to us. Maybe this is the new Nate, but I'm sensing worry?"

"We all love him to pieces, but since Sharon's death he's been the poster boy for all work and no play. It's like he's locked his emotions in a box and tossed it into the quarry."

Lauren glanced over at the man in question. "Looks like the coast is clear and from the scowl on his face, I'm betting he's not happy about what his mom had to say. Should we go offer aid and comfort?"

CHAPTER TWO

Nate looked down at his feet and rolled his shoulders. As his body gradually relaxed, he shook his head, his lips a thin line. No matter how good intentioned, his mom managed to push his buttons when she got on the topic of his love life. The problem was, she was right. It *was* high time he settled down, had that family he'd always wanted, little ones trailing after him, a wife waiting for him at home.

But the thought of what he could lose wound him up tighter than a Chihuahua in a crowd of strangers. Was it possible to care about a woman, live with her, have children with her, but be okay if life went south and he lost her? He couldn't survive being dragged back down into the dark, black hole of grief he'd been living in the past few years.

When he looked up, his heart did a rapid rat-tat-tat. Well, well, well. What have we here? His cousin, Crystal, was walking toward him and at her side was one of the most drop-dead gorgeous women he'd ever seen. She was tall, with a mass of wavy platinum blonde hair tumbling around a face that was at once sweet and sexy. And talk about curves. Sensuous enough to make a man want to get down on his knees and beg her to notice him, yet sleek and classy like a high-price race horse. He shoved the anxiety he felt at being pressured about his love life back in the cubby where it belonged. Maybe today wasn't going to suck after all.

When Crystal reached him, she gave him a quick, friendly hug, then stepped back and looked him up and down. "No obvious bruising, no blood, so it seems you escaped your mom relatively unscathed."

Nate's chuckle felt more like a piece of bread stuck in his throat than any humor at the situation. "You saw my mom?"

"Yes, and wisely kept my distance until she'd finished raking you over the coals. What did you do to piss her off this time?"

"She was chewing me out because I thwarted another one of her match-making attempts." He did his best to keep his tone light, like this was no big deal, but the assessing look in the blonde's crystal blue eyes told him he wasn't fooling her. Empathy and understanding radiated off her like the rays of the sun. Not his usual type, but if she wasn't looking for anything serious, he could see himself dating her and hopefully shift his mom's focus *off* his relationship status.

When it appeared Crystal wasn't going to add anything, the mystery woman discretely elbowed his cousin in the ribs. He knew it. Crystal wasn't standing in front of him by accident. He buried the inward sigh and kept his face neutral except for his brows raised in question.

Her moment of hesitation passed and Crystal launched in to what she'd come to do. "Nate, have you met Lauren yet? She's come to church with me a few times, but I haven't seen you lately."

"No, this summer's been crazy. Animals need attention when they need it and could care less about my plans. Now that Sue Ann has gotten her license and joined the practice, things should ease up a bit and I can get out more."

"In that case, Lauren Royall, meet Nate Kincaid."

He stuck out his hand and felt a jolt of pure energy travel up his arm as he enfolded her soft, delicate hand in his. "Nice to meet you."

"Likewise."

Her voice was soft, soothing, with a drawl he couldn't quite place. She looked him directly in the eye. This woman met life head on. Maybe dating her wouldn't be such a good idea.

"Lauren moved here a few months ago to join a marriage and family counseling practice and hasn't had time to meet many people," Crystal said. "Why don't you two find us a table and get acquainted while I grab food. I'm starving."

"You're always starving." Nate reached out and pinched her ribs. "Don't know where a little thing like you puts it all, but grab some for me while you're at it."

"You got it."

Nate hooked his thumbs in his front pockets and watched his cousin bustle away. Huffing out a breath, he muttered, "Is there any female in this family who *isn't* trying to hook me up?" Keeping his hands in his pockets he resisted the strange desire to go cave man and carry Lauren off somewhere. Instead, inclining his head toward the tables, he asked, "Should we find a place to sit?"

He felt her gaze on him and turned his head. The mischief dancing in her eyes made him feel alive and interested for the first time in a long time. Unease skittered across his scalp. He didn't want to feel attraction.

"I can't speak to Crystal's intentions, but I spotted you as soon as we arrived and asked her to introduce us."

"You did? Why?"

"You're attractive." She tilted her head and those lush lips formed a curious pout. "There's something about you intrigues me. I want to find out what." She shrugged. "I've made it a policy to let instinct guide me."

"Isn't that a bit risky? Acting without thinking it through?"

"Let me guess. You're an analysis and reason guy?"

"Yeah. What's wrong with that?" His body tightened and he stepped away. His tone sounded like a rusty hinge.

"Absolutely nothing. In fact I admire the trait. Sometimes wish I had a little more of it." Her head bobbed side-to-side in a carefree way.

"I sense a 'but' at the end of your sentence." He pulled out a chair for her at the long, folding table. Instead of sitting beside her, he moved to sit across from her. She made him skittish as a horse in a thunder storm, but an idea began percolating. He needed a fake girlfriend. She must be

11

unattached or Crystal wouldn't have introduced them. He'd think on that for a while. There was also something familiar about her, but he couldn't put his finger on it.

"We can find ourselves facing difficult, painful, even frightening situations, whether we carefully plan our lives or fly by the seat of our pants. Life has a habit of throwing us curve balls." She crossed her arms and lifted her shoulders. "The *going with my gut* approach has worked for me, but it's not for everyone."

Somewhat mollified, he decided to switch topics. "Where did you move from?"

"Raleigh, North Carolina, where I went to college, but home is Charleston, South Carolina."

"I thought I detected an accent. I like it. A different cadence than we're used to around here." He leaned back and crossed his arms over his chest. "Crystal said you're a counselor. Does that mean you're some kind of shrink or something?" Suspicion tightened his throat. Was his family sicking her on him to fix him?

He figured he'd stepped in it when she narrowed her eyes and with a quick movement shook the hair away from her face.

"Do you know how the term 'shrink' originated?"

He shrugged. "No, but I bet you're going to tell me." Yup, he'd hit a sore spot and a playful smile tugged at his lips. This playfulness was something else he hadn't felt in a while.

"In the field's infancy people used to think psychiatrists actually shrunk peoples' minds and started comparing practitioners to the aboriginal tribes that shrunk heads. It was as though the process of addressing mental health issues was somehow mystical and at the same time—nefarious."

"You don't say." Feisty—so unlike his fiancé's unflappable demeanor. Sharon had been steady and he'd always known what she'd been thinking.

"I do say." She rested her elbows on the table and propped her chin in her fists. She leveled a discerning gaze at him that made him want to squirm. "If people called you a 'quack,' how would you feel?"

A sharp pain stabbed him in the gut. "I wouldn't like it. I worked hard to get the education and training I needed to be a vet and I'm proud of what I do. I'm guessing the same applies to you. So how do you describe what you do?"

"My job is to help clients develop strategies to address whatever is holding them back from being the person they want to be."

"Basically, talking them down from the ledge?" Thoughtfully he ran his finger across his chin just below his lips and saw her eyes track the movement. She had to refocus before answering and a jolt of excitement made his breath catch.

"Sometimes the situation is critical and as you say, *we talk them down*." She leaned back in her chair. "But the vast majority seek therapy because *they* realize something is missing in their lives, things could be better, they could be better—and they *want* better. My goal is to help them find it. Does that help explain what I do?"

"I think so. You help people who need someone to hold their hands, instead of sucking it up and moving on."

"You don't think too highly of my profession, do you?"

He shrugged. "I can't imagine sitting around spilling my guts to a stranger."

"So if you felt like something was missing in your life, but had no idea what it was or how to change, you wouldn't want help trying to figure it out? You'd prefer to stay stuck?"

He grunted in response and shifted in his chair. "Are you always so certain you know what's best for other people?" She made him feel uncomfortable. He didn't like being reminded a big chunk of him was gone. He wanted the better she talked about but was he willing to risk getting it?

"So far my clients have been happy with their results, so yes."

"Hi guys. Sorry it took so long. I ran into Aunt Bootsie and she talked my ear off." Crystal plopped the tray she

13

carried on the table. "You two seemed deep in conversation. Glad you're getting along." She shuffled plates piled high with food in front of each of them along with beverages, napkins, and utensils. "Dig in."

Crystal served as a buffer and the conversation turned to safe topics like family, sports, ranching, and the weather. Lauren was charming, amusing, and intelligent. He liked her company and she intrigued him. His fake girlfriend idea just might work. He did have reservations though. Would dating a therapist—even if it was a superficial relationship—make him dig into parts of his life he'd prefer to ignore?

Once they'd eaten their fill, Lauren stood up. "I don't know about you two, but I'm ready for a dip in the pool. It's hot out here."

"I'm right behind you," Crystal announced.

At poolside, Lauren dropped her bag on a lounge chair then grabbed the bottom of her t-shirt, tugging it over her head. Her action exposed a smooth expanse of creamy skin that rippled softly with each movement. When Lauren shimmied out of her shorts, Nate's mouth went dry and his lungs stopped getting the message from his brain to breathe. Womanly perfection, hourglass curves, hips swaying like shore grass, she walked slowly toward the pool. When his brain cells started firing again, he couldn't move fast enough to catch up with her.

He shucked his shirt, kicked off his flip flops, and turned in time to see his own personal Aphrodite descend the concrete steps into the pool, trailing her fingers behind her. From the looks on the faces of the other males, he'd better join her quick. Three long strides and a shallow dive brought him face-to-face with this unwitting siren—and she splashed him. Laughing, she dove out of reach. He followed. They spent the better part of the next hour taunting and teasing. After he leveraged himself out of the pool, he stuck out his hand, to pull her out.

They walked over to where Crystal was sitting. She tossed them each a towel. Lauren rubbed her hair and wrapped the towel demurely around her body, tucking the corner in her bikini top to secure it. She looked up at the setting sun, the sky blazing in orange and yellow. He surprised himself by slipping an arm around her waist. He wasn't usually one for public displays of affection. He liked it when she rested her head on his shoulder.

His lips against her ear, he whispered, "Look, I intrigue you. You intrigue me. For once, I'm going with my gut. Do you like to country dance?"

"I looove," she drew the word out in a way that put a warm feeling smack dab in the middle of his chest, "country dancing."

"Good, then I'll call next week and set a time." He sure hoped he wouldn't be sorry about acting impulsively. One date didn't mean anything. If it worked out, he'd explain his predicament and see if she'd be interested in pretending to be his girlfriend.

CHAPTER THREE

It was after him. Snarling. Snapping. Terrifying in its ferocity. He couldn't run fast enough, his feet like lead as he moved in slow motion. It was gaining on him. Intent on dragging him into the depths of darkness to devour him. Capture the very essence of his soul and snuff it out.

Nate woke in a cold sweat, heart racing, his feet ready to hit the floor in flight. He sat up, disoriented. Leaning on his elbow he stretched across the king-sized bed reaching for the bedside table to turn on the lamp. His gaze took in the sand-colored walls, the weathered-wood furniture, and through the shadows to the master bath. Moonlight flooded through the window across from his bed outlining the branches of the oaks. He was in his bedroom, in his house, on his ranch. Safe. Secure.

It was only a nightmare. Another panic attack, but so real. The pain, the heartbreak of loss clawed at his chest. He'd thought he was past all this. Hadn't had one in ages. Could Lauren be the reason his bad dreams had returned? As busy as he'd been at work he hadn't been able to get her out of his thoughts.

Maybe he shouldn't have called her and arranged to go dancing. But he'd promised and he never broke his promises no matter what it might cost him. He'd thought he'd finally started to move on with his life. With sheer force of will he stuffed the nebulous fear back in its hole.

Sighing, he lay back down and prayed a dreamless sleep would claim him.

****

Nate's smart watch vibrated against his wrist. A message from his after-hours answering service blinked on the readout. He scowled. He wasn't supposed to be on call tonight. This was the first night he'd taken off in months. He and Lauren had just finished the first set on the dance floor and were heading back to their table for a beer. He'd been looking forward to spending the evening with her in his arms not out in a cold field or barn tending a sick or injured animal. But business came first.

"I need to return this call." He raised two fingers to the server and motioned to their spot at the end of a long trestle table. "I'll be right back." He walked out of the dimly lit room that hummed with hundreds of conversations and reeked of perfume, fried food, and beer to find a spot where he could actually hear his message.

His spirits plummeted faster than a skydiver hurtling toward earth. He clicked off his phone and tucked it into the clip on his belt. It was good the practice was busy, he had debts to pay and people who depended upon the work for their livelihoods.

He swiftly walked back and joined Lauren. Regret tightened his throat like a too-tight necktie. He hadn't brought up the idea yet that he hoped she'd help him fool his family into believing he had a serious girlfriend. Cutting their date short might decrease his chances of getting her to agree. Easing onto the bench beside her, he took a breath and dove in. He'd told her he had the night off and hated going back on his word, but he also couldn't shirk his duty.

"I have to go. A horse is in labor and needs help. The other two vets are already busy so that leaves me." Hunched over the table, shifting his beer glass back and forth in the condensation pooling on the table, he swung his head to look at her. "I'm sorry to do this, but I won't have time to take you home. Every minute counts in a situation like this. Can I call you a cab?"

She crossed her arms and rested them on the table,

looking at him with a frankness that didn't hold much promise. "No, I don't think so."

His heart clenched and he swallowed hard. She was going to dump him. He deserved it and already felt the loss. Maybe it was for the best to end things now if this is how he reacted to her after only one date.

A smile played around her tempting lips. "Take me with you."

"Are you kidding? You're all dressed up. You really want to watch a horse give birth?"

"Sure, why not? Life's only an adventure if you embrace new experiences. Come on cowboy, time's a wasting."

He captured her hand and brought it to his lips, relief pounding its way through his body. He sure hoped he wasn't getting in over his head, but for once he didn't care.

****

"Thank you for getting here so quick." The weather-beaten rancher with a jaw like a lantern and a gut that rounded above his belt, stuck out his hand. Nate shook it and clapped him on the back. He watched the man's eyes track to the entrance of the barn and his jaw drop. Nate ducked his head to hide his amusement. He knew what the sight of Lauren did to a man's thought process.

Is that your date?" the rancher whispered. "I'm sorry to interrupt your evening out."

"No problem George. Kincaid Veterinary Group *always* puts our clients first. Besides," he glanced over at Lauren and grinned, "She wanted to come."

He turned back to George, "Fill me in." Nate stood with his feet wide, his arms crossed, waiting for George to continue.

"She's been pacing which is normal, but she's been rolling on her back a lot which isn't."

Nate wrapped his hands around the stall bars and peered through to survey the scene. Clean straw on the floor, the mare's tail tied up, lights dimmed. As expected, the rancher had done everything right. Nate stepped back and flipped through this mare's previous birthing notes.

George lifted his hat to scratch his head. "I'm worried. Ruby here has given us some of the top cutting horses in the business. I'd hate to lose her or her foal."

"That's not going to happen on my watch." Resolve flooded Nate's system as determination kicked in. "How long has she been contracting?"

"The monitor went off about 45 minutes ago."

"Good thing you called. Let's see if we can figure out what's holding things up."

Nate turned to Lauren who had slowly eased closer to the action and offered up a lopsided grin. "Not exactly the way I pictured our first date ending. This could get a little messy. I don't imagine George will mind if you wait in his office down at the end of the barn." He glanced at George for confirmation. The older man nodded.

"For the record, Lauren Royall," she pointed to herself, "is no sissy. With a whole slew of brothers who put the dare in devil, I'm no stranger to blood." She rubbed her palms together and peeked into the stall. "What can I do to help?"

Nate wanted to kiss the living daylights out of her—but it was too public, too unprofessional. He settled for tugging a strand of her hair. "Okay. Buckle up buttercup." He squatted down, washing his hands in a small bucket of antiseptic solution and mild soap. Finished, he picked up the bucket and handed it to Lauren along with a tube of lubricant. "Follow me."

Lauren trailed behind Nate as he ran his hand along the horse's abdomen, his voice quiet and soothing. He grasped Lauren's free hand and moved her to one side, but within easy reach, slipped a shoulder-length surgical glove on up to his shoulder, and secured it by a loop over his head. "Would you squirt some of the lubricant on my arm?" He held out the gloved arm. She complied with quick efficiency.

After he'd finished the exam, he glanced at Lauren.

"Would you get two plastic gowns from my kit? And you might want to put those plastic booties over your boots. George, the foal is presenting backwards, but I think I can get it out without surgery."

From the expression on her face Nate could see she wondered what she'd gotten herself in to, but did as he asked. He stuck out his arms as she approached with the gowns. "Slip one on me and tie it in the back."

Once his was on, he held out the other gown for her and they repeated the process. He leaned down and whispered in her ear and felt her shiver as his breath tickled sensitive nerves. "Just remember, when you're sweaty, and dirty, and tired... I did offer to call a cab to take you home."

"What, and miss all this? Not on your life buster." Even though her smile telegraphed serenity, her eyes—twinkling like the stars filling the night sky—told him she was game for anything. She had guts, he'd give her that.

Hang convention. Nate kissed her quickly on the lips, then became all business.

"George, keep Ruby standing if at all possible... Lauren, I'll need you to help me get the foal to the ground once it's out. You may also need to help me pull." His orders were brisk, but calm. "I'll have to move quickly. Coming out backwards, the foal won't have oxygen until its head is free."

George looked down and shuffled his feet for a few seconds. When he looked up, Nate could see he was worried. "Will it be right in the head?"

Nate walked over to George, put a hand on his shoulder, and looked him straight in the eye. "Do you trust me?"

"Yeah," George nodded.

"Believe me when I say I'll do everything in my power to keep both mama and baby healthy. Okay?" The reputation of his practice depended on their success rate. Too many failures and he'd be out of business with debt up the wazoo. Anxiety swirled in his gut at the thought.

George nodded and pulled his shoulders back, ready to do his part.

"Everyone ready?" George and Lauren nodded. He rolled on a new glove and Lauren slathered more lubricating gel on his arm. "Here we go."

Nate reinserted his arm into the horse this time half way to his shoulder. "I can feel its hip and I'm moving my hand down its leg. Lauren, get the nylon strap with a loop on each end out of my bag."

She bent and looked into his birthing kit and pulled out a nylon strap. "Is this what you need?"

"Yup, that's it." Once the hoof appeared he reached for the strap and fixed one of the loops on the leg then handed the strap to Lauren. "Hang on tight. It *will* try and pull back and I need its foot to stay where it is until I get its other back leg out." Nate kept his tone soft and low. He repeated the process until the left foot joined the right. "Now I'll pull... Lauren, you need to help guide it to the ground." He looked over at her. "Ready?"

Lauren breathed deeply and nodded setting her stance to accept the weight. Within seconds the foal lay in the clean straw and a whoosh of fluid covered their gowns.

George grinned from ear to ear like he was a new father. Lauren, kneeling in the straw, clasped her hands to her chest a look of awe on her face. She tried to brush away an errant tear by rubbing her cheek against her shoulder. He knew exactly how she felt. The miracle of new life.

"Let's leave them be for a few minutes to bond." Nate stood, peeled off his glove, and put his hand out to help Lauren up. Gathering up his birthing kit and washing bucket, he motioned for everyone to follow him.

They all stepped out into the wide central aisle of the barn. Nate snagged two towels, handing one to Lauren so they could wipe their gowns. They stood silently for a few minutes, marveling at mom and baby lying peacefully in the stall. When the mare stood up to sniff her offspring and the foal began struggling to its feet, Nate removed his gown, helped Lauren out of hers and neatly rolled them before placing them, and the dirty towels, in a plastic laundry bag.

Lauren glanced back and smiled at him. Nate joined her at the edge of the stall.

"Does this ever become routine?"

"Never." He moved behind her, his hands resting on her shoulders. "Every birth and death is humbling. It makes me realize what a tiny piece of the universe each of us is, yet how important we each are in the chain of life."

Lauren turned to face him, cradling his face between her palms, and kissed him softly. "You are an amazing man and this was an amazing experience."

He hugged her quickly, then busied himself packing up his gear. He'd expected embarrassment at even that moderate display of affection, but it hadn't come. With his back to her he said, "You stayed calm under fire and didn't sweat the messy stuff. A lot of women would be worrying about their nails instead of the animals." He smiled at her. "And so far you haven't given me grief about cutting our date short."

Lauren walked up behind him, put her hands on his shoulders and leaned down to whisper in his ear, her voice silken as a river of warm chocolate. "Who said our date was over? The night's still young." She smiled and stepped back like she hadn't just said something that put the thought of hot nights and sweaty bodies in his head. "We could always stop someplace for a nightcap on the way home."

Nate felt his body contract from groin to throat and had to remind himself to breathe. In, out, in, out. Given the bulge forming in his jeans, other parts of his body longed to follow the advice he was giving his lungs. Her smile. Had it been flirty? Seductive? He couldn't tell. He couldn't read her. The first prickle of the fight or flight response tingled at the base of his skull. He turned his attention back to packing his case. He craved routine. Craved control over the chaos inside him.

Lauren stepped back, a puzzled frown on her face as though she sensed his shift in attitude.

Nate clicked the case shut, stood, and walked over to stand beside George. "I think we're about done here so we'll leave you to it. Call me if there are any problems. I'll stop by tomorrow afternoon to check on mama and baby."

The two men shook hands and did that man hug, back slap thing. Nate picked up his gear and turned to Lauren. "Ready?"

"Whenever you are." She fell into step beside him.

She stood next to him while he stowed his gear in his panel truck. Taking her hand, he walked her around to the passenger side and helped her in. It was the gentlemanly thing to do.

Before he could close the door, she cupped his face in her hands. In the overhead light, he could see worry clouding her clear blue eyes. "Are you alright? I get the feeling something is bothering you."

"Nope. I'm fine." He started to back away, but she tightened her hold.

"You're not fine. You shut down when I teased you in the barn about the night still being young. What gives?"

He lifted one shoulder. "I wasn't sure what you meant." Wariness crept into his gut and tension tightened his throat so his words came out raspy. "It sounded like... I don't know... like maybe sex is an option on a first date..." His voice trailed off. He wanted to pretend he had no idea why it would matter if she did offer sex on a first date. But he did know. His family wouldn't buy that he was interested in a woman who had a reputation for sleeping around. Besides, the man was supposed to make the first move.

"Okay, big guy." She tapped him in the chest three times with her index finger. "You need to work on your people reading skills. I *was flirting*—*not* inviting you to spend the night. And for your information, I don't have casual sex," she tapped him in the chest again, "but if it *had been* an invitation, there is nothing wrong with a woman making the first move."

Busted. Was he that transparent? "You can't blame a man for hoping a gorgeous woman might invite him to linger."

The serene and confident smile she leveled at him as she

settled into the bucket seat kicked him straight in the solar plexus, then shot down to his crotch. He braced his arms on the door frame feeling the need for support. "I am sorry. Sometimes my views are a little old-fashioned. Forgive me?"

"Yes, you're forgiven." Her steady gaze made him think she could see into the darkest recesses of his mind. "Forgiveness, of ourselves and others, keeps our Chakra in harmony." Her hands rolled in front of her as she took a deep breath.

"Never thought I'd date a woman who was in to that new-agey stuff." Nate pushed away from the truck and closed the door. He dug the keys out of his pocket and he climbed into the driver's seat.

"It takes a strong mind and body, grasshopper, to be our best." She rested her chin on her shoulder and playfully batted her eyes at him.

He laughed and turned his attention to the road.

"Are you busy this weekend?" he asked.

"Unfortunately, yes, but I'd like a raincheck. You owe me a do-over for tonight."

"True enough. Rain check it is. So, if you don't mind my asking, what's on your agenda?"

"My best friend is moving to San Antonio this weekend and will be staying with me until she finds a place of her own."

He pulled up in front of her house and came around his truck to let her out. Hand-in-hand they walked to her front door. Nate slid his hands under her jacket, trailing them down her ribcage before settling on her lower back. Pulling her tight, he wondered how one woman could set all his nerve endings on fire simply by being in his arms. He didn't know, and at the moment didn't care.

Their lips touched. He meant to keep it sweet, but his traitorous body had other ideas. Slowly he used the tip of his tongue to map the softness of her lips. When her lips parted to give him access to taste the essence that was Lauren, his resistance unraveled completely. Even while his heart raced, teasing her tongue, tasting her, she quieted him like the fading colors of the sunrise, heralding a promise of new beginnings. Were new beginnings even possible for him?

Her hands traced the contours of his chest, gliding across his hard planes, leaving streams of molten lava in their wake as they eased their way to his shoulders. Her arms circled his neck pressing her lush breasts tightly against him, tantalizing him with the thought of what they would feel like filling his hands.

Being wrapped in her arms was like being caught in a vivid dream, one he didn't want to wake from, but the gray fog of past nightmares swirled into the frame anyway. Shapeless and disquieting the fear lodged in his chest. The need to scurry into his protective shell took over.

He gentled the kiss, pulling back slowly, until their lips parted and he cupped her beautiful face in his large, calloused hands. Slipping apart, he felt his soul follow her breath into her body. Scared. Him. Shitless. He could lose everything—again, have to climb out of the abyss—again, if he stayed in her arms.

"I'll call you." He hoped his statement would be true. He wanted it to be true, but he heard the hollowness of his words. He felt her smile brush his lips and the heat it sparked as she melted against him. He was lost.

She sighed, her breath skimming along his neck, but when she looked up mischief sparkled in her eyes. "After a kiss like that, you've ruined me for other men," she whispered, her lips pursed at the laugh he suspected bubbled beneath the surface. "No other man can hold a candle to that kiss. That is a kiss for the ages. If you don't call, I'll probably die an old maid."

He choked back a laugh at her bantering. She always seemed to know what to do or say to lift the cloud of anxiety followed him like a beast of prey. "While I can't imagine you as an old maid, I certainly wouldn't want your spinsterhood on my conscience. I'll call. I promise."

Nate waited while she unlocked her door and stepped

inside. When he heard the deadbolt slide in to place, he turned and walked back to his truck still shaking his head, but with a smile playing at the corner of his mouth.

CHAPTER FOUR

A confident smile plastered on her face, Lauren walked briskly into the cheerful waiting area. She scanned the room, pleased with the inviting atmosphere they'd created for their clients. White wood trim accented pale, sage green walls. Several small groupings of overstuffed loveseats and chairs separated by half-wall partitions offered privacy in the large, rectangular room. End tables held small potted plants and popular magazines. A few long, narrow trestle tables topped with colorful flower arrangements and lamps nestled here and there around the perimeter. Decorative mirrors and soothing floral prints dotted the walls. The receptionist sat at a wooden desk at the back of the room rather than behind the typical glass partition.

Lauren approached the middle-aged woman and teenage boy sitting on one of the sofas and held out her hand. The attractive woman stood and smoothed her Armani skirt before accepting Lauren's hand. Makeup impeccable, auburn hair styled in a severe chignon, the woman looked stiff and unyielding.

"Mrs. Westbrook, it's nice to meet you." Firm handshake, all business, no hesitation Lauren noted.

Turning to the young man slowly coming to his feet, Lauren felt undercurrents of resentment rolling off her young client. His hair was neatly combed, his button down shirt pressed, and his slacks clean. From the look on his face, Lauren guessed his mother had dictated his attire and he was none too happy about it. "You must be Todd." She felt for the kid, and would bet a trip to the Bahamas, he wouldn't

27

want to show up to school dressed like this.

Limp handshake, eyes dull, and she had to lean forward to hear his quietly mumbled, "Pleased to meet you, Ms. Royall."

"Call me Lauren." She smiled at Mrs. Westbrook. "I'll spend the first half hour with Todd and then you and I can chat. Is there anything we can get you while you wait? Coffee? Tea? Water?" Lauren motioned for the receptionist.

"Water would be nice, but I thought Todd and I would talk to you together." Her face tightened causing the fine wrinkles around her eyes to deepen and her mouth to purse into a hard line. "The goal, after all, is to get past Todd's issues and begin functioning as a family again."

"Of course, and we will have sessions with you and Todd together—and your husband, whenever he's available. For now, it's most helpful to meet with you each separately so we can get to know each other."

Mrs. Westbrook glanced at her son, her frown deepening. "If you believe this is the best way to proceed, we'll trust your judgement. You came highly recommended." She sat down, her posture ramrod straight.

Lauren squatted down so she could look into the woman's face. "Thank you for the trust you've placed in me. I promise I will do my very best to help you deal with the challenges you're facing and bring balance back to your family's life." Commitment wove around her like a satin ribbon through braids. You had to earn people's trust in you every day, with every client.

Lauren stood up and motioned for Todd to follow her into her office.

Once Todd was settled in one of the padded accent chairs, Lauren started the assessment with routine ice-breaking questions.

"What year are you in school?"

"Sophomore." Todd looked anywhere but at her. She tapped her pen on her pad, drawing his attention back to her.

"What's your favorite subject?"

He shrugged. 'Don't have one."

"So school's not fun?" This was the hardest part of her job. A delicate dance between client and therapist. If she didn't get it right and create a connection, she wouldn't be able to help the person heal.

Todd shook his head.

"What do you like to do when you're not at school?"

"Play video games." His brows knit together in a scowl.

"What's your favorite game?" Lauren smiled. She could work with this. It was the opening she'd been waiting for.

"League of Legends."

"What level are you on?"

"Just reached 20." She could hear the pride in his voice. His jaw tightened and a hint of color tinged his pale cheeks. She figured he got grief at home for this.

"Impressive. So what role do you prefer to play?"

"You know the game?" His tone was skeptical. Lauren loved this part. Getting to know her clients, being surprised by them, and surprising them in return. The back and forth was like taking a trip to someplace she'd never been before, not knowing what she would find around the next corner. In her heart, she knew whatever it was, she could handle it. She always had so far.

"I played in high school and college," Lauren shared. "I preferred Dungeons and Dragons to the online games." Lauren smiled, remembering. "There's nothing like getting together with a bunch of friends to go on a quest and eat pizza. In League of Legends I'm partial to Janna. Who's your champion?"

"I'm a marksman and a Jayce guy." Todd shifted in his chair seeming to contract in before he looked up at Lauren. "I can see why you might enjoy D&D better, playing with a group of friends and all, but League of Legends gave me the friends I couldn't find anywhere else." He sandwiched his hands between his legs.

"What do you like about Jayce?" Lauren asked. Finally, she was getting more than one-word answers. The kid was like a lost puppy that Lauren wanted to scoop up and rescue, but she needed to keep this professional.

"He protects his people and is also wicked smart. He invents stuff. He's strong and can take a tower really fast, but you've got to have skills to play him. Once I mastered Jayce, I gave my team a real boost. Jayce makes me valuable, special." His eyes sparkled but his voice remained soft.

"I'm glad you've found friends who make you happy." She looked down at her notes. "Do you play any sports?"

"No." The answer came rapid-fire and final.

"Are you involved in any school activities?" Her eyebrows raised and she cocked her head, encouraging him to elaborate.

"No." Again the answer didn't invite follow-up.

"Tell me about your friends." Lauren kept her voice gentle. Soothing.

"My League of Legend team is way live. The five of us kick serious ass on a regular basis."

"Way live. Does that mean cool?"

"Yeah."

"I'll have to add that to my teenager translation files. These friends, you've only met them online?"

"Yeah." He shrugged in that teenage, defensive way. "So what? Online, in person, they're still my friends."

"I agree. People who support you and care about you are essential. Sometimes though, it's nice to be with someone you can actually touch and talk to without typing a message. Is there anyone at school or church you could hang with?"

"No." Terse and certain.

She tapped her pen against her pad of paper. "It sounds like your team respects your abilities and you have fun when you're with them."

"Yeah. They don't judge me." His eyes narrowed to slits.

"And everyone else *does* judge you?" Helping clients confront their issues made Lauren feel like she was back in South Carolina where the cloying summer heat made the air heavy and breathing difficult. Life just wasn't fair.

Todd exploded out of the chair. "I don't need this shit." He started pacing, his hands clenching and unclenching at his side, every line of his body rigid.

"You're right. You deserve to be respected and you don't feel you are. Is that why you tried to kill yourself?" Lauren's heart hurt, but she kept her manner neutral. If he sensed pity, she would lose him.

He stopped pacing. His head whipped around. "What do you know about me? You've probably read a file some dipshit wrote and you've talked to me for, what, 15 minutes. You don't know anything about me. Don't pretend you do."

Lauren could almost see the anger pouring off him like steam. Todd started pacing again. Her heart beat like the end of an intense workout without the euphoria that followed. Todd was so much like Patsy—isolated, unsure, believed he was unlovable. The adrenalin kick made her want to bound out of her chair, pace the room, but she used her yoga training to regulate her breathing and calm the anxiety clawing at her throat. Todd needed her focused. "You're right. I can't know you from reading a report and 15 minutes of talking, but I can see you're hurting. What would you change in your life to make it better?"

Todd stopped pacing, his hands stilled and his brow creased in a frown. "Huh?"

"You heard me. You're a bright guy. I think you know what's making you unhappy. So what would you change to make your life better?"

He dropped back down in his chair. "I want people to stop making fun of me. I want to fit in. I don't want to be gay and have everyone hate me."

"I won't lie to you and say our sessions will make all the bigots and bullies go away, that their words and taunts won't hurt, because that's not true. What you're going through is painful and that isn't going to change. Your response is the only thing you can control."

"Great, so the next few years, until I can get out of that hellhole, are gonna blow. Will what comes next be any better?" He bent forward and put his face in his hands— anger and emotion pushed deep inside. Lauren had to lean close to hear his whispered words. "I don't know if I can take it."

"There will always be people who ridicule others to make themselves feel superior. Too often meeting someone who is different—in your case, gay—causes certain people to behave badly." Lauren set her pad of paper and pen on her lap. "You do know that being gay is part of who you are and it's not something you can change?" She looked at him questioningly.

"Yeah, I know." His sigh seemed to come all the way from his toes. Bone-weary and soul-crushing.

"Good." She picked up her pad and made a quick note. "Has your school counselor talked to you about the school's anti-bullying policy?" She'd storm the school and make them see reason if they hadn't. Too many schools still didn't understand the important role they played in preventing bullying.

"Yeah, but I don't want to be a snitch. That would only make things worse."

"Is there anyone at school who takes your side or at least seems concerned about how you're being treated?"

"Not really. Everyone's afraid of being bullied."

"I'm sorry you don't feel safe at school. I'll talk to your counselor to see if she has any ideas for stopping the harassment." She made a note to call the school to learn more about how they reached out to students. She'd be happy to volunteer to help make presentations.

"I don't want to start any trouble. Things are bad enough," Todd said.

Lauren could hear the fear in his voice. "I know, but your school has a responsibility—and it's a law—to protect its students." She ducked her head trying to catch Todd's eye. Having the chance to make a difference, not only in this young man's life, but the lives of other students, filled her with a sense of purpose and power. "Have you heard about the gay teen youth group in town?"

"No."

"Okay, here's your homework for our next session. First, I'll email you the group's contact information and let them know you'll call. They meet every Tuesday evening. I'll talk to your mother about making sure you have a ride to the meetings. You onboard with that?"

"Whatever." But he nodded.

"Second, I'll email you links to a few videos I want you to watch. They were made by people who are now adults but who realized they were gay as teenagers. They want you to know, life will get better. I expect you to write down what you learn and how that makes you feel. We'll review everything when we meet next week. Third, I want you to keep a journal of times when you feel like you can't take it anymore and what happened right before. I'd also like you to write down when you're happy and what happened to make you happy. What you write in your journal is only for you, unless you want to share."

She reached over to her desk and handed Todd a hardcover journal and pen. "Can you do that for me?"

"Do I have a choice?" He jerked his head to flip a strand of hair out of his eyes.

"We all have choices, but I'm wagering you want things to improve. Agreed?" She put out her hand as she stood up.

He stood and slowly offered his hand in return. "I guess."

They walked to the door. "Take a seat in the waiting room while I talk to your mom. Mrs. Westbrook, won't you join me?"

CHAPTER FIVE

Lauren swept open her front door and launched herself into her friend's arms almost knocking the petite beauty over. Giddy and laughing, the two hugged tightly before holding each other at arms-length for the obligatory once over.

Ashley pushed her sunglasses to the top of her head, pinning her long mop of wild black curls away from her face. "You're looking good, girlfriend. San Antonio obviously agrees with you. I wish you'd let me take you shopping, though. We need to get you out of those god-awful yoga pants and into something a bit more chic," Ashley said.

"Why?"

With a '*you have to ask*' look, Ashley rolled her eyes. "Are you sure you were born and raised in the South? I declare, if I didn't know better, I'd swear you were dropped in from another planet." She hugged Lauren again and added, "And you know, as your best friend, anything I say, is said with all love and respect."

Lauren grinned. Like fine champagne, Ashley's personality sparkled. Slinging one arm across her friend's shoulders, she steered her into her modest, three-bedroom, ranch-style house. "I love you to death, but I *like* the way I dress. It's comfortable, and suits me. I'll save my high-fashion moments for when I'm modeling."

"You're right. What you wear suits you, and come to think of it, I wouldn't want you to change. Ignore what I said. It was just vestiges of my mother casting her judgmental shadow." Ashley shuddered. "May I bite my tongue every time I sound like her. Besides, even dressed like a hippy, you make all the rest of us look like poor church mice."

"Says the woman who turns men's heads wherever she goes." Lauren snorted. "I like to think it's the woman, not the physical appearance that captures a man's attention."

"Maybe in some alternate universe." Ashley snickered and dug a finger into Lauren's side. "Truth or dare. What do you notice first about a man—his amazing personality or his amazing body?"

"You are *so* annoying." Lauren scowled down at her pal and assumed her most haughty model pose. "I'll leave it to fate to point me to the man I'm meant to be with At this point my career is more important than any man."

Ashley followed Lauren into the open concept great room. "I like what you've done with the place. Comfortable, colorful, but definitely not the Zen I expected," Ashley said. She pivoted taking in the distressed wood flooring, large oriental area rug between two cushy sofas in soft floral prints, and house plants everywhere. "The open concept and all the natural light is wonderful."

"Most of the Zen décor I've seen is ultra-modern, and just not me." She held her hands palms up near her shoulders and shrugged. "I like colorful and squishy, eclectic furniture. I'm complex. What can I say?"

"You never were one to conform to a stereotype." Ashley dropped her purse on the floor next to a sofa.

Lauren walked over to the French doors and let in her Golden Retriever who immediately wriggled against Lauren's and Ashley's legs. Ashley crouched down and ran her fingers through the dog's silky fur.

"She's not the puppy from the photos anymore. Her name's Honey, right?"

"Yup, she's my sweetie." Lauren ruffled the dog's ears then sat on one of the sofas. She patted the cushion beside her, motioning for Ashley to sit. Tucking their legs under them, they twisted to face each other. "I'm glad you're here. Skyping and Facebooking isn't the same. I hope this will be the fresh start you're looking for. It's high time you put yourself first."

"Says the woman who wants to solve everyone's problems and puts herself last," Ashley said.

"I never said I didn't have some things to work on too." But at the moment she couldn't think of a thing she wanted to change – she had her independence, work was rewarding, and, even though she wasn't looking for a relationship, Nate had potential for a fun time. "So when does your stuff arrive?"

"The truck should be here in about an hour." Ashley scrunched up her shoulders and grinned at her friend, happy energy swirling around her like a mini tornado. "So tell me about this Nate guy, the one who brought you along to help deliver a horse." She shook her head in disbelief. "Never would have thought *that* would put a twinkle in your eye."

Lauren took a deep breath. "You know better than anyone, most of the guys in my life have been friends. A few made my heart go thumpity thump, but never fireworks. Nate's like a fourth of July extravaganza."

Ashley nodded. Lauren couldn't believe she was going to say this, but remembering the first sight of Nate turned the butterflies loose in her belly again. "You know that old cliché about a couple spying each other across a crowded room, and you instantly know this could be the one?"

Ashley smiled. "Yeah, I do. You always thought that was a bunch of baloney."

"Not anymore." Lauren flutter-patted her chest. "I looked at him. He looked at me. Instant sizzle."

"Okay!" Ashley clapped her hands together several times quickly. "Now we're getting somewhere. Good for you!"

"It's exciting and scary at the same time. This kind of intense, immediate attraction is new to me. I was beginning to think I was like Mother Teresa—great love for humanity, but no soul mate. While that never bothered me before, now I'm wondering if I've been missing something." A flicker of doubt floated into her head. A person could focus on her priorities and still have a serious relationship, right? Love didn't have to mean you gave up being yourself. At least she hoped so.

"Oh, my goodness. You're blushing! *You never blush.* I gotta meet this guy. Does he have any hot friends?" Ashley slapped a hand over her mouth. "No wait. Scratch that. After Bill, I've sworn off men." She grimaced and sighed, slumping in dejection. "No I haven't. I've only sworn off the lying, cheating scum of the earth variety, so count me in if Nate has any hot, *nice* friends."

Lauren unfolded herself from the sofa and stretched down to touch her toes. "Want some tea?"

"Sure," Ashley bounced up, "but keep talking," she said as she followed Lauren into the kitchen. "I want details." She made a 'come on' motion with her hands. "Must be quite a guy to get you all hot and bothered. You never fell for any of the dreamboats you met modeling."

"It's hard to put my finger on it. Maybe that's why I'm still interested. He's a bit of a puzzle. Plus there is an undeniable sexual attraction. When I walked into that barbecue and saw him—tall as an oak tree, muscles rippling under a thin t-shirt—oh, my goodness." Lauren sucked in a breath and fanned her face with her hand. "My senses were dinging like a wind chime in a hurricane." She sighed. Was this really her, sounding like a love-struck teenager?"

"He has the most gorgeous eyes. Steel blue that focus on you like a laser. Granted I don't have much to go on with only one date and the barbecue, but when he's with me, *he's with me.* He's not like a lot of guys staring at their phones and ignoring the person they're with." A pout formed on her full lips. "Although if a work call comes in, all bets are off."

Lauren held the tea kettle under the faucet then set it on the stove to heat. She snagged two mugs from the cupboard, and a selection of herbal teas and a jar of honey from the pantry before sitting next to Ashely on one of the high kitchen stools along the counter.

"Sounds like a keeper to me," Ashley squirted honey into her mug and rummaged through the tea choices. "What's the catch?" Ashley smacked her head with her palm just as the kettle started to whistle. "What am I saying? If he puts the toilet seat down, what *are* you waiting for? Snag that man."

"Wouldn't know about the toilet seat yet." Lauren said as she pulled the hot water off the stove and poured the boiling water into their mugs.

Lauren perched back on the stool, idly dunking her tea bag as thoughts swirled through her head. "I get the feeling there's something he's not telling me."

"Sweetie, he's a man. There's probably a lot he's not telling you and there's a good chance he doesn't even know what it is he's not telling you."

"My gut tells me he knows what's bothering him, but is trying to bury it. Not healthy." Lauren squished the tea bag against her spoon then placed the bag on a saucer. Finally a guy who made her want more than a casual fling and she couldn't figure him out. One minute he was all over her, but two minutes later he'd back away faster than a dog with its first whiff of skunk. Irony crinkled its nose at her. Talk about role reversal. Usually guys did the chasing and she did the slowing down.

When the doorbell rang, they both stood and headed for the living room. Over the next hour, two burly men paraded in and out delivering the sum total of Ashley's worldly goods. It didn't amount to much since she only kept her bedroom and office furniture, kitchen stuff, her dishes, a few linens, and being the Southern gal she was, an extensive collection of clothing. The furniture easily fit into the bedroom Lauren had designated for Ashley, but the boxes of clothes meant standing room only until they were unpacked.

After the movers left, they worked in companionable silence, dancing around occasionally to a favorite tune or singing off-key to the chorus. A half hour later, Lauren shoved three empty wardrobe boxes out the door. Ashley zipped her suitcase shut and stowed it in the closet then opened a box of linens. She pulled out her sheets. Lauren watched her hug them tightly to her chest, inhaling deeply of the potpourri-scented fabric. Her friend was still suffering and Lauren knew she'd do whatever it took to help her friend heal.

Ashley plopped an armload of sheets on the bed and walked over to hug her friend. "Thank you so much for putting me up for a while. It makes starting over a little less scary."

"I'll always be here for you. Besides, It'll be fun being together again. It's been too long—since the summer before college. Where *did* the last ten years go?"

"We were busy. College, master's degrees, professional certifications, first jobs." Ashley flopped onto the bed her arms spread wide. "Living life."

After they shoved the last box into the hallway, they surveyed the room. Ashely sat on the bed smoothing the comforter on either side of her with her hands, a far-away look in her eyes. Lauren sat down beside her.

"You've been put through the wringer lately," Lauren said. "Bill did a real number on you."

Fine lines of sadness etched Ashley's forehead and shadowed her eyes. "I just don't seem to learn, though I will admit, Bill took the lying, cheating bastard thing to a whole new level." She sighed. "And, of course, Mother thinks the breakup *was all my fault.*"

Lauren slid off the bed and knelt in front of Ashley, a fierce protectiveness heating her cheeks. "Ah, sweetie, your only fault is being too trusting, and a little too eager to please. We both know your mother makes devil mom look like a saint."

Ashley smiled sadly. "Why can't she love me for who I am?"

Lauren wished she could smash the woman in the face, but that would be bad karma. Breathe and focus on what Ashely needed. "Because she is who she is—manipulative, controlling. You need to give yourself permission to be *who you are* and stop trying to be the person *she* wants you to be." Lauren patted Ashley's knee. "We'll work on that while you're here."

"Do you really think I can stop feeling guilty because she disapproves of me?"

"I *know* you can. I've worked with lots of clients in a similar situation. They made it to the other side, and so will you." She'd do as much as she could anyway. Being so close to the situation made complete objectivity impossible.

"I envy you your confidence. I wish I felt even half as sure I'm in charge of my destiny as you do." Ashley looked at her quizzically. "Do you ever question yourself?"

"Of course I do. Everyone wonders about decisions they've made—and whether they've made the best one." Lauren squared her shoulders. She was a trained therapist. She knew how to help people now. Not like before. "In my work, I've seen results and have made a difference in people's lives. That's one of the reasons I'm so sure about the advice I offer." She'd been tops in her class giving her a firm foundation for believing in her skill as a therapist.

"So you've forgiven yourself?" Ashley's brows rose in question.

"What do you mean?" Lauren had a sinking feeling she knew what Ashley was referring to. The one time she hadn't listen to what her gut instincts were telling her.

"It wasn't your fault Patsy was raped. As you're so fond of saying, 'people hear what they're ready to hear.'"

"But if I'd tried a little harder, instead of focusing on who would ask me to the prom…" Lauren felt the regret to this day.

"You did try," Ashley interrupted. "You told her Ben was no good, even if he was the most popular boy in school. We were in high school, the age of invincibility. She didn't believe you. Her rape and suicide is not on you."

"My mind knows you're right, but my heart wishes for more. It's hard for me to accept I did enough." If truth be told, that's why she'd gone into counseling—to prevent another Patsy. It's why she'd worked so hard in school and during her internship to become the best therapist she could.

Patsy's death had changed her life. A part of her free-spirit personality had died that day, replaced by a determination to hear cries for help and to do something about them. She wondered if the desire to fix people's problems was one of the reasons she was drawn to Nate. If that was the case, she needed to keep a professional distance.

Lauren sighed and stood up. "What's say we get the boxes of stuff you don't need into the garage and go get some dinner?"

"Perfect. Here's to new beginnings." The two high-fived as they headed out of the room.

CHAPTER SIX

Lauren's butt swayed enticingly with each stride as she moved up the trail about five paces in front of Nate. All those womanly curves in his sightline put an entirely new perspective on what it meant to enjoy nature. If she were simply a pretty face, he could date her a few times and forget her. Turned out, he liked her as a person. When she greeted him, a smile lit up her face and he got a warm tingle in his chest. When he tried to retreat into himself, she teased him into the here and now. Compassionate, loyal, intelligent—and if he were honest—he envied her spirit of fun and adventure. He'd always done what was expected of him. Maybe he could stand to have his world shaken a little. Like a dab of salad dressing made it better, and too much made it a soggy mess.

The crunch of boots on the trail, the smell of juniper and wild sage mingling with damp earth from yesterday's light rain, the dogs—his and hers—frolicking between them then charging off into the brush, was the perfect way to end a busy week. She filled a space he hadn't admitted needed filling. With her, his dreams of a life with Sharon faded into the mild fall sunshine—at least temporarily. Today he would give himself a pass and live in the moment. He hadn't even glanced at his phone in the past hour. That was a first, but one he knew he couldn't indulge in often. A balloon payment on his second mortgage was due soon.

He picked up a small, fallen branch from a Thornless Honey Locust tree and used its feathery leaves to tickle her neck. She turned and smiled. His heartbeat paused. A little

42

Googling uncovered why she'd looked so familiar when he met her. She'd started modeling as a teenager and still did on a part time basis. She's spectacular. No wonder advertisers clamored for her to hawk their wares. He caught up with her and took her hand.

"I'm glad you called, otherwise I would have hiked alone today," Lauren said. "After the first week went by since we'd seen each other, I was beginning to wonder if we would see each other again."

"If you recall, I did ask you out, but Ashley was moving in." His brows drew together and he squeezed her hand. "You would have hiked by yourself? That doesn't sound wise. You didn't have any friends who would join you?"

"Sometimes I just want the chance to commune with nature. Lots of people think they have to fill the silence." Lauren touched his arm in the way Southern women do when they want to blunt a criticism. "Don't get me wrong, I love my friends, but your strong, solid, quietly-assured presence fits my mood today."

"Are you trying to tell me *I'm not* the life of the party?"

"Let's just say I haven't seen that side of you yet."

"You wound me." He placed a hand to his chest. "I have my sensitive side." He did, didn't he? He hadn't completely buried it. He continued to write in his poetry journal almost every day.

"Do tell?" she said.

The flirt and sass in her voice and eyes interrupted the messages between his brain and feet causing him to stumble over a rock in the trail. Heat flooded his face. He had to dig deep to remember he had a sensitive side and not let loose a string of curse words. She was going to think he was an idiot. He wasn't usually klutzy around women. Why Lauren? Because he liked her?

She stopped walking, crossed her arms, and stared into his eyes with an intensity that made him want to squirm. "Personally, I think you like being the grounded, responsible one. The one your brothers and friends turn to. You like being in control."

"Maybe, but don't go trying to use any of your psychological tricks on me." He wanted to bite his tongue the minute the words left his mouth. She lengthened her stride, making it clear she was not pleased. He didn't like the heavy lump that settled in his chest or the impulse to beg forgiveness.

They walked in silence until Lauren stopped, gasped, and pointed. "Oh, look."

Nate rushed up and assumed a fighting stance, alarm in his voice. "At what!"

"That bird." She choked back a laugh. "It's a Black-Capped Viero. They're on the endangered species list so you don't see many of them anymore."

"Jeez, you scared the life out of me. I thought you saw a snake or something."

"Really? A big guy like you is afraid of a little snake?"

Color heated his neck followed by relief. At least she didn't appear to still be angry at him. "Safe to say I have enough respect for the critters around here to know I don't want to step on one." He envied her the ability to shrug life's irritations off. He should apologize for belittling her profession, but he didn't want her getting too close.

About 50 yards down the trail she moved onto a wooden deck and rested her forearms on the railing. Turning her face to the sky, she closed her eyes, basking in the warmth of the late fall sun.

Nate unzipped his sweatshirt, leaned his butt against the railing, and studied her. Absently scratching the ears of his German Shepherd, he wondered if the reason he'd fallen in love with Sharon was because she was comfortable, he knew what to expect, no surprises.

"Feels like you're a million miles away. What's going on in that head of yours?" Lauren asked, her eyes still closed and face pointed at the sun.

He shrugged. It was easier to talk when she wasn't looking at him. "You may be right. I'm the oldest. Don't know whether its nature or nurture that makes me the way I am. It was *my job* to watch out for my brothers and younger cousins. I had to *prevent* the shenanigans, not instigate them."

She shifted beside him and he felt her gaze on his face. "Could be a little of both. Most of us aren't all one or the other, but some combination of personality and life experience. I suspect that's not the reason your head was someplace else. Want to talk about it?"

Nate grunted and pushed away from the railing. "Let's head back and get lunch."

Lauren looked at him curiously. "That's the end of our conversation? No plans to wax poetic on the deeper meaning of life?"

"Nope." He hoped the tightening in his gut didn't show in his face because she was quick to pick up on body language. No way was he going to let her start scratching below the surface. *He knew he'd loved Sharon and they would have had a happy life together.* She'd been his rock—practical, gentle, and predictable—the perfect partner. Lauren was so different or was she? Both women were inherently kind, liked being outdoors, and would be the first to jump in and help someone in need. Sharon's spirit of adventure wasn't as pronounced as Lauren's, but it was there. She'd been the first to encourage him to follow his dream and set up his own practice. Emotion clogged his throat. He still couldn't think of Sharon in the past tense.

He started to move away, but Lauren grabbed him. "Wait. We need to take a picture. Commemorate the moment."

His feet felt heavy, a war raging inside him over his growing attraction and the equally strong urge to push her away. Commemorating something felt too permanent, but he did as she asked and stood beside her.

"Oh, come on now. Get a little closer."

She snuggled into his side and he had to admit it felt darn good. He took her phone, stretched out his arm, "You ready." She nodded and did a Daisy Mae pose—boobs pushed forward, knees slightly bent, and eyes big and innocent. He wondered how she could look both sexy and demur at the same time.

"Thank you," she said when he returned her phone. She fell into step beside him, snapping her fingers and calling to her dog.

He traced his fingertips along the column of her neck. She was like catnip. A slight tremor ran through her at his touch. She was attracted to him and he was attracted to her. If he moved forward with asking her to be his surrogate girlfriend, could he keep an emotional distance between them? The dark growl of fear sent him into retreat mode. He had to shut her out until he figured this out. "Come on, Bear. Let's give you a little exercise." Snapping his fingers, he started off at a brisk trot with his dog at his heels.

****

Lauren set the basket she'd retrieved from her car on the table and started pulling out containers. She felt Nate's presence behind her. The tightness in her chest eased when he plunked a small pail filled with sunflowers on the table. She hated being out of sorts with people. Made her feel like a piece of jerky inside—tough and without flavor unless you added it. "Your sensitive side?" she asked, a hint of humor in her voice.

He shuffled back a few steps and shoved his hands in his pockets. "Yeah, I guess. Look, I'm sorry I was a jerk. I don't know what gets in to me sometimes."

"Sometimes talking can help us figure out why we react the way we do." He crossed his arms over his chest. Stubborn man. As if asking for help to deal with his issues would suck the life out of him. She closed the lid on her picnic basket and stowed it under the table. Lauren picked up the pail and held it at arm's length. "I love sunflowers. How did you know?"

"You seem like a sunflower person. Cheerful, colorful, carefree." He ducked his head and looked down at his feet like he'd said too much.

"You're a walking contradiction. One of you brings me flowers and the other turns his back on me. One minute I think you like me and the next I feel like a leper." She took a breath and plunged ahead. "Are you playing some kind of game?"

"No, no games. Gun shy, maybe. Getting too close to a woman can open a man up to a world of hurt."

"And you've been there, done that?" His expression closed and she immediately missed the carefree man he'd been before she'd hit whatever nerve had made him flinch. She wanted that relaxed man back.

"Yeah, but I'm not ready to talk about it."

"Fair enough. What *would* you like to talk about? It's a beautiful day. We've enjoyed each other's company. I'd like to keep it that way." She'd find a way to tease out happy Nate or die trying.

"Well I do have something on my mind. A problem you might be able to help me solve."

He had the look of a fox approaching the hen house. He wanted what was inside, but wasn't sure what might be lying in wait. She put a smile in her voice to put him at ease. "I'm listening."

"My family's been bugging me about finding a steady girlfriend. They seem to think I'm afraid to get serious about anyone." He picked up one of the containers and lifted the lid.

"*Are* you afraid of getting involved?" She didn't expect him to open up but thought it was worth a shot.

He sniffed the contents of the container and put it back down. "No, just haven't found anyone I want to date on a steady basis."

He swallowed hard and looked away. Nate was lying, What part was the lie—that he hadn't found anyone he wanted to date or that he was afraid to get involved? "What can I do to help you solve your problem?" she asked.

"I was thinking, maybe you and I could date, like we're a

couple, so my family would back off."

A spark of annoyance flickered in her chest. He wanted people to think they were a couple but didn't really want to *be a couple*. "Let me see if I understand. We'd date. We'd *pretend* to be serious about each other but it'd really be casual?"

"About sums it up." He ran a hand through his hair. "I like you. I think we have fun together and when my family decides I'm not avoiding having a serious girlfriend, we can still be friends. You interested?"

"We do have fun together and since we're both concentrating on our careers, a serious relationship isn't something either of us needs." She stuck out her hand. "You've got a deal."

"Good." He shook her hand. "What is all this stuff?" He indicated the food.

Silly man thought this was the end of their discussion. She'd let him deflect—for now. "This one is turkey and avocado wraps. I also packed fresh vegetables and humus, fresh fruit kabobs, red potato salad with yogurt dressing, and double chocolate brownies."

"Except for that last thing, it all sounds kinda healthy." She saw the suspicion in his eyes. "I brought my portable grill." He lifted the lid of the basket. "Don't suppose there are any hot dogs or hamburger patties in there?" His expression shifted to hopeful and she had to bite her lip to keep from laughing.

"Only what you see." He looked like he was being sent to the principal's office. She put something from each container on his plate and nudged it toward him. "Who knows, you might learn there's more to eat than steak and potatoes." Getting him to step outside his comfort zone and knock some of the rigid out of his spine would make a good first step in his road to recovery.

"I eat other stuff, but I like what I like," he grumbled.

Parking himself on top of the picnic table, his feet propped on the bench seat, arms resting on his knees, she knew the moment he resigned himself to humor her. His chin dipped, his shoulders sagged, and he picked up a turkey wrap between two of his large fingers like it was a dose of castor oil. He slowly moved the food toward his mouth, opened wide, and bit down. She also knew the moment he discovered he liked it. Yes, another victory. She wanted to fist pump the air, but refrained because nobody liked a showoff.

His eyes closed and a satisfied hum throbbed low in his throat. He swiped a baby carrot through the humus and popped it into his mouth, chewing slowly to savor the flavors. He eased a melon ball off the kabob stick with his teeth. How could a man make the simple art of eating so arousing? Moisture and heat gathered at the apex of her legs.

A predatory grin spread across his face. The man was toying with her. He ran his tongue along a strawberry, slowly capturing it between his teeth before easing it off the skewer and into his mouth. The movement created a slow burn in her center. As he continued eating, the flames licked higher, tinging her cheeks with blush. Her fingers itched to tangle in his hair. Very deliberately, his tongue teased the corners of his lips. He took her hand and pulled her to stand between his legs. His hands smoothed up her arms. How could a simple touch be so magical? He cupped the back of her neck then eased her forward for a kiss.

Firm, full lips slid over hers drawing her into a boiling pool of lust and want. Strong arms pulled her tight—the only thing keeping her tied to earth when she longed to float, to soar, to experience everything that was Nate. His other hand spanned her waist a fistful of her shirt in his grasp. Lauren leaned into his strength. More, more, more ran through her mind. This felt... so... good.

"What the hell," Nate cursed. "Nothing like 60 pounds of demanding dog squirming between us to drag a guy back down to earth." He glared at the unrepentant animal. "Honey, you've got rotten timing." Nate stood, moving Lauren to the side, and took a few steps back, a flush creeping up his neck. If he was embarrassed to be seen with her, why did he want her to be his pretend girlfriend?

He scrubbed his eyes with the heels of his hands. "Maybe I should thank Honey. That kiss was a little too intense for public consumption."

She reached over and stroked a hand down his arm. "It's okay. I get it." His admission added another layer of insight into how his mind worked. The man was uncomfortable getting too lovey-dovey in public. Could this be another tool he used to keep from getting too close?

He joined her on the bench. Leaning to nudge her with his shoulder, he said, "I get carried away when I'm around you. Why is that?"

Her eyebrows furrowed then relaxed. Curious. "You're a closet Casanova and can't always hide your passionate nature?" She shrugged.

He smiled like she knew he would. "You got me." Nate rubbed his jaw. "It would seem I haven't had much adventure in my life." He elbowed her gently in the ribs. "Tell me something wild and crazy you've done."

"I don't know if you can handle it."

"Try me." He picked up her hand and brought it to his lips. The sexually charged banter acted like a spark plug, igniting a longing to have more.

"All I'm going to say right now is, me and Ashley. Sophomore year in college. Spring break. Daytona Beach." She placed a finger under his chin and pushed his mouth closed. "Here have another turkey and avocado wrap."

"You went there? Two women alone?" His voice sounded like they'd done a Thelma and Louise and driven off a cliff.

"Sure did." She propped her chin in her hands. "You never went on spring break in college?"

"No. I usually worked on getting my practical training hours in during spring break or helped my dad at the ranch." His lips quirked in a half smile. "Seems like I've always been dedicated to duty." He bit into one of the brownies. "These are amazing." He studied it before popping it in his mouth and scooping up another. "So where are you off to?"

"I do volunteer work at the children's hospital. I need to get home and change. Today I'm in charge of a puppet show for the kids."

"I'm impressed. Every time I think I have you pegged, you surprise me." He scooped up the picnic basket and slung an arm across her shoulder as they walked to her Honda CRV. She pulled out her car remote and popped the hatch so Nate could put the basket away.

She cupped his face in her hands and kissed him sweetly on the lips. "Call and let me know when you want to start 'operation fool the family'. Just so you know, my schedule is crazy over the holidays. I'll be hosting my family for Thanksgiving week and will be attending a conference right after that. For Christmas I'll be in South Carolina. Maybe we should wait until the new year to get started?"

"I agree. I've got a cousin's out-of-town wedding to attend and I put in more hours at the clinic in November and December so others can take time off." He opened her car door and placed a hand on her shoulder.

Electric sparks tingled all the way down her arm like she'd touched a live wire.

"We should be seen together sometime over the holidays so people start thinking of us as a couple," Nate said scratching his head. "We have a company Christmas party. Maybe that will work."

"Send me the details and I'll be your official 'pretend' date." She still wasn't sure how she felt about this idea. As a psychologist she saw so many ways this could go sideways. Deception was not in Nates wheelhouse. When he looked at his cousins and their young families, it was all over his face how much he envied them. Hopefully spending time with him would give her a chance to delve deeper into his relationship issues.

CHAPTER SEVEN

Lauren leaned against the meticulously refurbished 1955 Chevy truck and breathed a sigh of relief. Another messy scene—starring her best friend—diverted. They guy Ashley had dated since moving to San Antonio—the one who had cancelled their date because he had to work—was inside dancing with another woman. Ash sure did know how to pick them. Standing in the chilly parking lot of a popular dance hall having a heart-to-heart about the fickleness of men was not what Lauren had pictured for this evening.

Granted she was having her own man problems. She and Nate had one date after the holidays and let it be known they were a 'couple.' Tonight made over two weeks since she'd heard from him. Not that he had to call, but a relationship—even a pretend one—put certain expectations in a woman's mind.

Both women looked up when they heard the crunch of gravel under booted feet as two men walked toward them.

"Lauren?"

Nate. She'd know that voice anywhere. It looked like he had time to go prowling with his brother, but no time for her. She knew it was pride talking—another one of those things she wanted to work on—but that didn't stop her blood from boiling.

Nate stepped closer and tipped his hat back peering into her face—invading her space. "It is you. Are you alright?" He clasped her arms, a flash of concern, then quickly stepped back like he'd been burned. "What are you doing standing around in a dark parking lot? You could be mugged or worse."

"My friend and I needed a quiet place to talk. We're perfectly safe." He may be a take charge guy, but he wasn't going to take charge of her. She took a deep, calming breath. If she was going to take part in this farce and act like his girlfriend, then Nate needed to step up. "Hello Nate. Long time no see." Lauren did her best Greta Garbo imitation. From the look on his face her zinger hit its mark and he had the good grace to wince. She pivoted slightly and faced Nate's brother. "Hi Zach, nice to see you again."

"Always a pleasure," Zach drawled as he gave her a hug before focusing his attention on Ashley. "Unlike my brother, I'm thrilled to find two beautiful women dropped into my path. "Like herding cattle he managed to maneuver Ashley away from Nate and Lauren.

Lauren bit back a smile. She guessed Zach came by his ladies' man reputation honestly.

Nate stepped closer. "I'm sorry I haven't called. One of our partners has been out with the flu so we've been shorthanded. I should be home tonight catching up on my sleep, but Zach can be mighty persuasive." He tried to stifle a yawn as he reached out and gathered her hand in his huge one.

Lauren pointedly withdrew her hand and stepped away. Instead of the disappointment raging inside her, she hoped she looked cool and detached. "Work before pleasure. Nice to know where *your girlfriend* stands in your list of priorities."

"That's not fair," Nate said. "Would you put me before your clients?"

"No, but my professional life doesn't take *all* my time. I make sure I have a life," she hissed. She turned her back on him, closed her eyes, and willed herself to relax. This wasn't her. Putting a hand to her stomach she pressed at the unfamiliar roiling. Nate had been busy. The poor guy looked like he needed a break.

Zach and Ashley set off toward the dance hall deep in conversation. Nate held back. Lauren sensed the man had something he wanted to get off his chest.

She sighed and turned to face him. "I'm sorry, that was out of line. Sounds like you had a rough week." Her hand cupped his cheek. "I'm a little confused about how this thing between us is supposed to work."

He put her hand in the crook of his arm and they walked toward the dance hall. "I guess I hadn't thought it through."

Lauren forced her words past the tightness in her throat, keeping her tone as accommodating as she could. "If we're supposed to make people think we're a couple, then doesn't that mean we're," she cleared her throat, "exclusive."

His step stuttered. "That would make sense."

She rolled her eyes, glad he couldn't see them in the darkness. "I'm willing to go along with this charade, but I also don't plan to sit at home waiting for you to take me out. I like to do things. That means, at least until you have your family off your back, you need to make time for us to be a couple." She couldn't fault him for putting work first, she just didn't want him to put work first all the time.

"Agreed. I promise I'll do better."

"In that case, we should probably get to know each other better," she said. "I'll start."

"I love the night sky in Texas. So many stars." Lauren tilted her head back and scanned the sky as they walked letting the universe breathe into her soul.

"I can't imagine a sky not filled with stars. The only place I've ever been outside the Southwest was a year in the Dominican Republic with the Peace Corps. I must admit, they have pretty spectacular night skies, but nothing compares to home."

"*You were in the Peace Corps?*" Her head whipped around.

He flashed a devilish grin, making her insides all quivery. "I'm not as plain vanilla as *some people* think."

"I think you're more like salted caramel—surprising."

"Salted caramel. I like that. The sweetness of heaven, mixed with the salt of the earth."

"That's very poetic." Drip by steady drip his charm

melted her heart. She'd been attracted to him from the first time she saw him. Now she wanted to find out whether or not this—whatever this was—could be real. Looking for a serious relationship hadn't been part of her plans, but when presented with a fork in the road, a person needed to make a choice. "So what made you decide to go into the Peace Corps?"

"I wanted to have a meaningful impact on people's lives. I figured once I started building my practice and settled down I'd miss my window of opportunity. Helping people in developing countries with agricultural and animal husbandry projects brought home how fortunate we are to live where we do."

"And here I thought you weren't open to new experiences," Lauren said. Nate had a huge heart, one of the things that attracted her to him.

"Doesn't exactly make me a thrill-seeker, but it was adventure enough for me." He pushed back his Stetson and glance over at her, his eyebrows arched in question. "Am I still in the doghouse?"

"No, I can't stay angry with people. Grudges equal negative energy. Negative energy drags a person down. I don't want to be that person."

"*I really was going to call.*"

"We're together now. That's a start. Let's enjoy the moment." The here and now, that's what she believed in—or at least that's what she told herself. "I suspect we'll make the rules up as we go." She also suspected doing so would be a challenge for him.

Nate held open the massive wooden door on the old store-front building. Lauren walked past him, saying goodbye to the fresh night air and his spicy cologne and hello to a place humming with excitement.

Framed photos of past performers dotted the walls on both sides of the narrow entry. On the left just past the entry, a bar and small dining area carved out a niche. Straight ahead lay the dimly lit cavernous dance hall. The band was in full swing and couples were two-stepping their way around the hardwood dance floor, their boots creating a staccato rhythm. She felt Nate's hand at the small of her back ushering her toward a table. Tingles of awareness like cat's paws crept up her spine. It was all she could do not to shudder at the pleasure of his touch.

Zach, the more gregarious of the brothers, took matters in hand. "We'll go check your coats and round up some drinks. What's your poison?"

"Corona," Lauren and Ashley said in unison.

"Ah, ladies after my own heart. Here, let us help you with your coats."

Nate stood behind Lauren, his hands resting on her shoulders as he removed her coat. His lips brushed her ear as he whispered, "I'm glad I came tonight. All of a sudden I'm feeling energized. Not tired at all."

He turned and headed off in the direction of the bar with Zach. Lauren watched him move through the room. People giving way like he was the lead bull in Pamplona.

"Not bad, girlfriend," Ashley high-fived her friend. "I can see why you decided to go along with this fake couple thing. His brother's not bad either." Ashley sat on the bench seat and Lauren joined her. "Do you think it's going to work?"

"Who knows?" Lauren angled her head close to Ashley's so the two could hear each other over the din. "I like him and when he's not shutting me out, he's fun to be with. We actually have a lot in common."

"Such as?" Ashley's foot bounced in time to the music.

We're close to our families, loyal to friends, want to do things that give our lives meaning." She held out one hand, palm up. "Then there is the other side of Nate…" Lauren put her other hand palm up. "Those things that drive me crazy." "He's the tiniest bit inflexible." She held her index finger about a quarter inch from her thumb. "He likes order and hates bending rules. That's why I'm surprised he suggested this."

"Take it from one who knows. He is who he is. You

aren't going to change him."

Lauren chuckled, "Since this is a temporary thing, I have no intention of changing him. I'm hoping I can help him work through his issues. Getting him to loosen up would be nice too, make his life less stressful."

"If your goal is to loosen him up, you ought to get him out there doing yoga with you." She elbowed Lauren in the ribs.

Lauren gave Ashley a 'get real' look. "Is that so I'll stop bugging you to join me?"

"Possibly, but I bet he'd look hot in spandex yoga pants."

Heat spiraled up Lauren's neck at the image of Nate in spandex. The pair of conspirators looked at each other and dissolved into a fit of giggles.

"I do hope we're not the butt of some joke." A deep voice rumbled like an ancient god from on high.

Lauren looked up at Nate with her most innocent expression. "Why of course not, darlin'. I'd only laugh with you, not at you."

"In that case, here's your beer." He settled on the seat next to her. Arm to arm, thigh to thigh, she felt pricks of awareness at each point of contact.

"Did I tell you yet, you look mighty fine?" Nate's words stirred the loose tendrils around her ear and pinged into the pleasure center of her brain. He leaned close and sniffed. "You smell good too." He stood up, set his beer down, and offered her his hand. "Want to dance?"

Lauren put her hand in Nate's and stood up. "I thought you'd never ask." His lips curved in a grin that would make her agree to anything. "Come on cowboy. Let's show them how it's done."

As soon as they hit the outer ring of dancers, he twirled her, then pulled her tightly against his chest before launching into a country two-step. The exhilaration of moving as one, the charge she got from his touch was like a lightning strike zapping her, creating a buzz from head to toe.

The band shifted to a cha-cha beat, giving her the chance

to shake and wiggle what God had given her. The look in his eyes burned like a wildfire. The attraction sizzling between them was hotter than a cast iron skillet. They were in the middle of a Country Waltz, lost in the dreaminess of the tender movement, staring deeply into each other's eyes when she felt Nate startle and glance over his shoulder. Zach motioned for them to follow him out of the flow of dancers.

"I want to take Ashley for a late-night breakfast and was wondering if you could give Lauren a ride home?"

"Sure. No problem. You two kids have fun. Now scram." He twirled Lauren and they smoothly transitioned back into the haunting, 3-step Waltz, letting their bodies do the talking.

When the band took a break, he asked, "You ready to head home?"

Lauren nodded. Her hand nestled in the crook of his elbow, his hand covering hers, they walked to the coat check area. Nate discretely kissed her neck as he helped her into her jacket, causing shivers of desire to run down her arms. When they reached his truck, he opened the door, putting his hands on her waist to steady her while she climbed in. She appreciated the consideration he showed and the cared-for feeling she always got with him.

After they pulled into her driveway, she asked, "Would you like to come in? I made a batch of lemon squares this afternoon." She crossed her fingers, hoping he'd say yes.

"I'd like that."

Once inside her kitchen she asked, "Would you like tea or coffee to go with dessert?"

"Coffee would be great."

He followed her and settled onto one of the four tall stools lining the kitchen bar. While Lauren got the coffee and dessert ready, Nate absently fiddled with a spoon pushing it so it spun on the counter. She laid her hand over his.

"A penny for your thoughts?" she asked.

He took a long sip of his coffee. Put the mug down. Picked it up and took another sip. She waited, giving him the time he needed to say what he had to say.

He scrubbed a hand over his cheek. "You've mentioned a few times that I start to get close and then pull back." He stared into the depths of his coffee as though looking for words. When he looked back into her eyes, a muscle twitched along his jaw. "I can see why you'd think that." He took another sip of his black coffee. "I guess I'm just not quite over the death of my fiancé." He shrugged.

"Oh, Nate, I'm so sorry. I'd heard about your loss. You must have been devastated."

His hands tightened around his mug and she feared it might shatter under the pressure of his powerful hands. "Devastated, that about sums it up. People tell me I've grieved long enough and it's time to move on. I guess they're right and *I am trying*, but moving on doesn't feel right… yet."

"There is no time table for grief. Only you know when you're ready." She hoped he wouldn't close down, but wanted to plant the seed. "I gather you've never spoken to a counselor?"

"No. Another one of those things that doesn't feel right to me."

"If you ever do decide to talk to someone, the owner of our practice, Jasmine Masters, is really good. I think you'd like her."

He grunted. "I wanted you to know, the problem's with me, not you."

She squeezed his hand. A warmth flooded her system and her chest felt like a pressure valve had been opened. He was beginning to trust her. "How did she die?"

"Brain tumor." He started to fidget again, shifting his weight on the stool, looking uncomfortable and ready to bolt.

"You must miss her a lot. It's hard to watch someone you love suffer. I'm guessing this isn't something you want to talk about right now." Every fiber of her being longed to ease his pain. If nothing else Patsy's suicide had taught her people needed to address their pain to keep it from turning into tragedy.

He shook his head.

She moved the dessert plate closer to him. "Have a lemon square and tell me why you became a vet." She watched him relax. Better she thought.

"My Grandpa Kincaid was a vet. From as far back as I can remember, I followed him everywhere and begged to be taken on rounds. Caring for animals was like breathing. I knew that's what I wanted to do."

He took a bite of the sweet lemon morsel. "These are amazing. Almost tied with the brownies you made."

"Thank you." She smiled and sipped her tea. "So what do you like best about being a vet?"

"The chance to take something broken and make it better." He was a different person when he started talking about what he did. Passionate, alive, eyes glowing, voice vibrant. She wanted him to be like this all the time.

"That's similar to why I went into counseling. Only with me it's people instead of animals."

He stifled a yawn. "I need to be on my way. I have surgery first thing in the morning and for some odd reason they expect me to be awake and alert."

"Go figure." She ran her fingers softly across his stubbled cheek. "I hate to see you go, but we both have places to be early tomorrow morning. I'm seeing a high school student before school starts."

They both stood and she linked her arm through his, cozying up to him as they walked to the front door. He slipped on his jacket then tugged her into a snug embrace. His mouth, sensual as easing into a fragrant bubble bath, staked a claim on her heart. From deep in her brain, recognition bloomed like a rare flower, seldom seen and more cherished for its rarity. She felt as fluid as chocolate left in a hot car, melting against him. She could get used to this.

His arms tightened—one across her back, one on her butt—fusing their bodies from chest to thigh. Sensations, new and vital, swamped her leaving her adrift in a sea of passion tossing her this way and that, exhilarating in its wildness. She felt his need pulse against her belly. How she wanted to satisfy his need. Now. Always.

The kiss intensified, tongues teasing, dancing, finding pleasure in each other's lips. Her hands framed his face holding him to her, urging him to take what he wanted. Breathing turned ragged. His hands moved to cradle her face as he broke the kiss to stare intently into her eyes, searing her with his gaze until she thought she would melt into a puddle.

"I want to make love to you, but I can't go there yet. You're not someone I can easily forget. When I make love to you, I'll be making a promise with my body and want to be sure I'm ready to keep it. I need more time before I can do that."

He leaned his forehead against hers. "You sure do test a man's resolve." He picked up his hat and placed it on his head before giving her one final, sweet kiss. "I'll see you soon. You can count on it. I'll also give some thought to talking to your partner."

Lauren leaned against the door after he left, her thoughts racing. It felt so right to be with him... but did he feel the same tug of primal recognition? Lust for sure, but was there more? When he let his guard down, more seemed possible. Funny how life works. A month ago, her focus had only been on building her practice. While work was still her top priority, maybe there was room to have balance in her life.

CHAPTER EIGHT

"Thanks for driving today. I'd completely forgotten that my check engine light came on. Guess I can't put off a trip to the mechanics any longer." Lauren twisted in her seat, a hint of contrition whispering through her head. "I admit, there are *some* drawbacks to my lack of organizational skills."

"Breaking news." Ashely held out her phone like a microphone. "Care to elaborate?"

Lauren playfully swatted it away.

"Changing subjects," Ashley said, "While it was nice the Kincaid men pitched in and helped me move to my new place yesterday, Nate sure had a poker up his butt. Do you really think he believes all the stuff he spouted about men's and women's roles?" Ashley spared her friend a quick glance before returning her attention to the road. "I know this boyfriend thing started as a lark, but if you're falling for him, like you said, do you really think it could work between you?"

"I don't honestly think he believes what he said. Whether or not we can share something special?" Lauren shrugged. Was she sure? Her instincts said yes. She was beginning to wonder if he said the things he did to keep her at arm's length to protect himself. He knew she had a much looser interpretation of how men and women built a life together. "On the flip side, he grew up believing men are the protectors and breadwinners—women the nurturers and homemakers." Uncertainty sat heavy in her gut. Could getting involved with Nate change who she was as a person?

"Being raised on a Texas ranch I guess his views shouldn't surprise me, but I always expect guys our age to be more…"

"Contemporary?" Lauren suggested. "He is. Below the surface beats the heart of a softie. He looks for the potential in people." A look of frustration crossed her face. "I do wish he respected what I do for a living though. It hurts that he thinks it's all a bunch of nonsense." Lauren sat back, arms crossed, and a frown puckering her lips.

Ashley slowed, glancing up at the huge metal letters spelling out 'Rocking K' on the sign arching over the gravel road angling off the main road. "Is this our turnoff?"

"Sure is. About a mile farther down we'll reach the ranch compound."

Ashley's head swiveled right and left as they traversed between fenced pastures. "Is all this Kincaid land?"

"Yup, both sides of the road as far as the eye can see." Lauren leaned forward to peer out the windshield. "Crystal's family has the next ranch up the road and Kincaid uncles and cousins own more land in the area. It's so beautiful out here." Lauren relaxed against the soft leather seat. If she were ever to put down roots, this would be the spot. Roots didn't mean a person couldn't be free. Plants kept stretching and reaching for the sun—unless bigger plants blocked out the sun and they shriveled and died. She wouldn't let that happen.

Ashley approached the main compound of the Rocking K, and slowed.

Lauren motioned Ashley to pass the main hacienda and keep going toward the ranch-style home about 300 yards farther on. "See all the cars over there? That's Zach's place. Apparently he has the biggest television."

Zach skipped down the front steps to greet them as soon as they stopped. He engulfed Ashley in a warm embrace and steamy kiss. Now that's how a man ought to greet his special lady.

Lauren nodded politely during Zach's introductions to the other guests, but everything was background noise except Nate. Every fiber of her being zeroed in on him. His gaze locked on hers as he unfolded from the sofa and ambled toward her.

"Glad you could make it today." He leaned in, gave her a quick kiss on the lips, and put his arm around her.

Game on. Let the couple show begin. Patting his rock-hard abs, she slowly swept her hand across the spot she'd just patted. A smug grin spread across her face at the heat that leapt into his eyes. He might think they were play-acting, but he was also attracted.

Nate's mom uncurled with the grace of a matriarchal tigress and stalked over to where Ashely and Lauren stood. Before they knew it, Gloria June had one arm around each of their waists crushing them tightly to her side.

"I'm thrilled to have a few more females to balance out all the testosterone in the room," she said in her husky contralto before she started barking orders. "Zack, quit gawking, and go put those pans in the kitchen. Father, how is that grill coming? Nate, quit hanging on Lauren, and go help your father. You men folk take all these youngsters with you. Let them burn off a little steam before we watch the game."

The assembled males sprang to attention, shoved kids into jackets, and hurried out the back door.

"Ladies, I believe we have work to do in the kitchen." She hung on to Lauren's hand and held her back as the others headed for the kitchen. "Lauren, can I have a word with you?"

Her gracious smile eased the butterflies fluttering in Lauren's belly, but ramped up her curiosity. She nodded wondering if Nate's mom knew about their charade.

"I can tell my son's taken a shine to you, and I'm thrilled. First, you seem like a sensible woman. Second, Nate's had a hard go of it and he's skittish as a new colt. It's encouraging to see him with someone." Gloria June paused. The look on her face left no doubt she was measuring Lauren against an internal yardstick—the one all mothers pull out when looking at someone their offspring might be interested in. "Has he told you anything about his fiancé?" Gloria June sat on the sofa and Lauren joined her.

Lauren's insides felt as squishy as a wet sponge. She didn't like deceiving people—another trait she and Nate shared. "Only that she died of a brain tumor about three years ago. He's worried he should be ready to move on, but isn't. I get the feeling he's afraid of getting hurt again." Lauren captured her bottom lip between her teeth, uncertain how much to say to the mother of the man who was starting to mean so much to her. She sure didn't want to get off on the wrong foot.

"That's about the size of it. He and Sharon started dating in high school. Early on, they both wanted to be vets and spend their lives together doing what they loved." Gloria June twisted and propped one booted foot on her knee. "She was a few years behind him in school. While she finished up, he joined the Peace Corps. They thought they were on track to live the American dream. Life had other plans. When Sharon got sick, Nate moved heaven and earth to get her the best care he could. He borrowed heavily against his clinic and ranch to help her family pay the medical expenses. He's just now getting his head above water."

"There's more to the story, isn't there?"

Lauren could see Gloria June was choosing her words carefully. "I suspect he's carrying around guilt that he went off to the Peace Corps—did something that was important to him—and lost time he could have spent with Sharon." She tapped a finger against her lip before continuing. "He doesn't have a selfish bone in his body, but he's beating himself up that he put himself first… for once."

"I suspected as much." Not only was he afraid of having his heart ripped out of his chest again, but this kind, generous man felt like he'd let down the woman he loved.

"I know you haven't been seeing each other long, and I don't want to scare you away, but I thought you should know where he's coming from." Gloria June put her hand on Lauren's knee and look intently into her eyes. "Granted, I see him through a mother's eyes, but Nate's a keeper, strong and steady as they come."

Lauren put her hand on Gloria June's. "I agree. *He is a special man.*" She hesitated, not wanting to offend. "I suggested he meet with a counselor I know. Sometimes it takes an outsider to help us recognize what's going on in our heads so we can make changes."

Gloria June slapped her hands down on her knees and stood up. "Beautiful and brilliant. I'm glad we had this talk. I'll do what I can to back you up." She hooked her arm through Lauren's. "Now, let's go join the others."

When they entered the kitchen Ashley was sprinkling toasted coconut over the cake she'd brought and one of the cousins was sliding casseroles into the oven. Amid friendly chatter, food was readied, carted into the dining room, and squeezed on to the massive oak table. Chips, salsa, bean dips, salads of all kinds, Texas chili, spicy chicken wings, burgers topped with jalapenos, and a mountain of desserts jockeyed for position.

Everyone gathered around the table and bowed their heads for the blessing. As soon as 'Amen' sounded people loaded food on plates and found a spot in the great room to watch the game on the enormous flat screen television that occupied most of one wall. Nate's arm draped across her shoulders, snugging her tightly against him. This was the definition of happiness. She fell right in to the easy camaraderie and yelled at the refs for bad calls—meaning any call going against the Dallas Cowboys.

At the end of the game, Gloria June began collecting dirty dishes. "Ya'all know cleanup would go a lot faster if everyone got off their butts and pitched in."

Booted feet hit the floor as men, women, and children scurried to do the matriarch's bidding. Forty-five minutes later, the place was spotless except for several stacks of dishes that needed to be put away. Gloria June disappeared and reemerged with several jackets in her arms.

"Nate, that stack of dishes belongs in the main house. You and Lauren can cart them back for me… and Nate, that doesn't mean leaving them on the kitchen counter for me to put away."

"Yes, Ma'am." Lauren could almost hear his boot heels click together as the big bear of a man snapped to attention. She hid her smile by busying herself piling the smaller dishes into a rectangular wicker basket on the counter.

Nate plucked their coats from his mother's arms, shrugged into his, and held Lauren's out for her to slip into. His hands smoothed over her shoulders, firm and promising. He turned and loaded the rest of the dishes earmarked for the main house in a large roasting pan. With the pan cradled against his hip, he used his other hand to open the door for Lauren. "Shall we?"

Lauren picked up the basket and they set off on a well-worn path, lined by solar lights between Zach's house and the main compound. The friendly banter of ranch hands returning to the bunkhouse drifted on the cool, early evening air.

His free arm slipped around her waist. Lauren savored the instant tingle shooting through her at his touch. She stumbled and Nate pulled her close to steady her. He looked at her lips. He lowered his mouth to hers. The tingle turned into a 5-alarm fire. Was that low moan coming from her? Him? Both? He tried to align their bodies to increase the contact, but the load they carried made that impossible. He huffed out a frustrated sigh. She knew exactly how he felt.

Nate straightened, letting his fingertips trail down her cheek and trace a line along the collar of her jacket. She had a strong urge to purr with pleasure.

"The sooner we dump this stuff, the sooner we can engage in some serious canoodling," he said.

"Did you just say canoodling?" Laughter bubbled in her chest like a pot of boiling water.

"Yeah, it's something my grandpa used to say. It just slipped out. Won't happen again." She loved the teasing in his voice. Wanted more of that.

They walked into a kitchen designed to cook for a small

army. It was equipped with two wolf ranges, a set of built-in double ovens, three refrigerators, two freezers, two commercial dishwashers, and a long table that would seat at least twenty. Despite the size, the space had a homey feel – lace curtains, colorful cushions on the chairs, and cookie jar and bowl of fruit on the counter.

"I hope you know where all this stuff goes."

He looked around the kitchen and she could read the uncertainty in his face. "Sort of. We'll mostly have to open cupboards and wing it."

"Something tells me your mama isn't going to like it if we make a mess of her kitchen," Lauren muttered as she started opening doors. "Hand me those two lasagna pans. I think they go here." She rolled her eyes as his hand hovered over various options. "Those two yellow, rectangular, ceramic pans."

He picked them up and stood behind her, pressing into her, scattering slow kisses up her nape. "Tell me where you want me to put these." His words whispered into her ear as he captured her between his body and the counter. He blew at a stray wisp of hair, then ran his tongue along the sensitive spot below her ear.

She shivered in delight. "Put them anyplace you want." Her voice husky with desire, Lauren turned in his arms, linking her hands behind his head. The pans clattered as Nate hastily nestled them on the shelf.

Their lips fused. Her mouth opened inviting their tongues to dance. He tasted of the after-dinner mint he'd had and smelled of some woodsy, spicy, citrus scent. His 5 o'clock shadow marred her delicate skin. A not so discrete cough interrupted them.

Nate eased back and glanced over his shoulder. "Hi, Mom. We're getting the dishes put away just like you asked." He picked up a stack of plates.

"Uh, huh." Gloria June gave her son *that* look. "Better duck because pigs are flying." She chuckled. "Zach is giving Ashley a tour of the barns. Why don't you two join them…

and try and stay out of trouble? I'll finish up here."

"Are you sure?" Lauren asked. "I hate to leave you with this mess."

"I knew you were a sweet gal. Nope, you two go on."

Nate grabbed Lauren's hand and planted a quick kiss on his mother's cheek. "Thanks, Mom."

They walked into the barn hand-in-hand, shoulder-to-shoulder, heads together, laughing at a shared joke. Right this moment, she wanted it all—a successful career as a therapist *and* a life with Nate. Confidence surging, all things were possible when she set her mind to it. He'd be an amazing dad for all those kids she wanted someday.

Nate spotted his brother and Ashely locked in a steamy embrace. "If we're interrupting something, too bad,"

Lauren punched his arm. "Ow! What was that for?" he said, rubbing the spot she hit.

"For being a really annoying big brother," Lauren chided, "and for turning back into that comic book superhero with the shield and major do-gooder attitude. Leave them alone."

"What's wrong with him?" Nate drew back in shock. "He's my hero. How can anyone possibly question an American icon?"

"Nothing's wrong with him. He's a fine, upstanding citizen, but he can be a bit stuffy. He needs more laughter in his life." And that's the medicine she vowed to give to Nate.

Forehead to forehead with Ashley, Zach said, "I was just giving Ashley a tour of the operation."

"Really? Are you showing her the operation or the operator?" Nate smirked, but used his hand to protect his shoulder from Lauren's wrath.

"Funny," Zach countered his voice sarcastic. "Ashley wanted to see the horses. Now I'm getting ready to take her out back and show her the rest of the facilities." Zach held up his finger to stop his brother. "Don't go there. Since Lauren hasn't seen the place, why don't you two join us?"

"Love to." Lauren angled her head toward Nate who was reading a message on his phone and frowning.

"Don't make a liar out of me." Irritation struggled to get a toe hold in her happy day.

"Huh?" He looked up.

"I bragged you were one of the few men I knew who stayed present instead of burying himself in an electronic device. Am I wrong?" She crossed her arms. Work is important, but everyone needs time to step away and focus on self. Nate, with his penchant for seriousness, needed that time more than most.

"Sue Ann did her first solo surgery yesterday and I was checking for updates." He must have picked up on her exasperation because he shoved his phone back in its holder and looked contrite. "But right now I'm more interested in getting friendly with my favorite lady." He spun her around so her back was against the wall. He braced his hands on either side of her head and leaned in.

"Smooth move, doc." His smile whispered against her lips in a most seductive way as his hands slid down to circle her waist. A feather couldn't fit between their bodies. Her world became his breath flowing across her cheeks.

"We want to make sure everyone believes what we're selling. I got more moves. Wanna see?"

"Oh, yes, please." Pretend or not, she planned to enjoy the moment. This is the person Nate hid under layers of isolation.

The kiss started out gentle, but quickly grew serious. His hand cupped her butt and snugged her into his growing erection. Her hands linked behind his neck holding him tightly in place. Her breasts pressed against his hard chest, her nipples pebbled, aching for his hands to caress them. Was this what sky diving felt like? Floating free, the air rushing in your ears and a falling sensation in your stomach as you plummeted toward earth.

"And over here," Zach said loudly, "is our veterinarian treatment room. Nate, you want to give Lauren a private tour? Ashley and I can go on without you?"

"I think we all ought to stick together," Ashley said.

"Safety in numbers. Come on you two lovebirds."

Nate shifted back and their pulse rates slowed.

"Are you sure you're not part witch? Every time I'm around you, I feel like I'm possessed."

"To the best of my knowledge, no witches in our family tree, but I know what you mean. You're like a drug I can't get enough of."

"Are you two coming or not?" Zach hollered.

"Yeah." Nate took her hand and kissed her knuckles one-by-one.

A half hour later Ashley looked at her watch. "Much as I've enjoyed today, it's getting late and tomorrow's a work day. Lauren and I need to get going."

Nate turned Lauren to face him and looked over his shoulder at Zach. "You two go on. We'll catch up with you in a minute."

After Zach and Ashely moved off, Nate said, "Whenever I'm around you I don't know whether I'm coming or going. I'm sorry when I push you away, but today, at least, the urge to run didn't kick in."

"I'm glad because I enjoy being with you." She kissed her finger and placed it on his lips. "Don't be a stranger."

They walked to the car and he opened the door for her. Bending down, he kissed her softly. Lauren turned as they pulled away from the ranch and was pleased to see a smile on Nate's face.

CHAPTER NINE

Nate leaned back in his office chair, his boots propped on the desk and a patient file resting in his lap. Two of his partners—Wayne and Sue Ann—along with his youngest brother Josh, walked in the office. While his partners settled at their desks, Nate stood and exchanged a back slap embrace with his brother.

"What brings you out to the clinic?" Nate asked as he sat back down in his chair. Josh parked himself in the visitor's chair in front of Nate's desk. "Where's Chad?"

"He's with his mom today so I thought I'd come out and check on the new software program I built for you. How's it working out?"

"Like a dream," Sue Ann said. "It's made a *huge* difference."

"Yeah," Wayne added. "I didn't realize how much time we wasted before. Our lives are so much easier now with all our records in one place. You're a genius."

Nate smiled at his brother's discomfort. "Don't make his head swell. He's hard enough to live with." He had to admit that the Kincaid brothers could stand reinforcing news to bolster their spirits. Zach couldn't convince Ashley he wasn't a playboy and she should take him seriously. Josh was getting crushed by his divorce. Nate was beginning to think of Lauren as a fixture in his life and that wasn't part of the plan. What a mess.

Sue Ann answered the phone and Wayne started tapping away on his keyboard, intently staring at some bit of information on his computer screen.

Josh angled his head at the two empty desks. "I know Paul's still on his honeymoon, but where's Mr. T?"

"You know he hates that nickname. One of these days he's gonna get you." Nate shook his head. "He's out on a date with Lauren's partner, Jasmine." He wasn't sure how he felt about one of his partners dating the counselor Lauren had suggested he see. He brushed the unease away. Wasn't there some kind of oath to ensure she couldn't talk about patients with anyone? Wouldn't make any difference though if he never followed up.

"How'd he rate a day off?"

"Theory is we're all supposed to get two of them every week." Nate stood up and retrieved his field equipment bag. He couldn't complain since he had the coming weekend off for his family's rodeo – or so he hoped, barring emergencies. "Come on, walk with me. I need to check on one of our new mamas."

"Mamas, plural?" Josh followed his brother out the door.

"Yup, three right now and one on the way. It's been busy around here." Yet another Saturday down the drain. He huffed a breath through his nose. Lauren was being a good sport about his schedule. "So how are you holding up? When's the divorce final?"

"Not sure. Finished the social worker's visits, but need to wait for her recommendation to the court. My lawyer says Cindy doesn't have a chance of getting sole custody in the temporary order." Josh clenched his fists. "One thing I *can* tell you, it's either shared custody or I get sole custody." He lifted his hat to scrub one hand across his wavy, brown hair. "How do I feel? Like I've been hit by a Mack truck." He scowled at his brother. "If you tell anyone I said that, I'll have to kill you."

"Yeah, you and who else, lil' bro?" Nate hooked his arm around Josh's neck in a mock choke hold.

Josh planted a fist in Nate's diaphragm and the air whooshed out. "I could ask you the same question. How are you doing? Isn't this about the time of year Sharon got sick?"

Nate's hand gripped his equipment case like it was a life preserver thrown to a drowning man. "Three years ago today she got her test results back. Eight months later we were holding her funeral. Should have been celebrating our second anniversary next month." He slid open the barn door and they walked inside the dimly lit corridor. A dull ache settled under his breastbone. The nickering of horses and the scent of hay helped ease the tightness inside him.

"Question still stands."

"Better than last year. Still feel like I've had all the air sucked out of me, but now I remember how to draw a breath."

Nate stopped in front of the stall door, inhaling deeply and letting it out slowly until he felt his body relax. Looking down at his feet, he spoke softly. "Gotta calm myself so I don't upset the mama and her baby, but to answer your question, I finally think I've moved past the darkest place."

He unlatched the top half of the stall door. This was his element. Here he was in control. The two men leaned their forearms on the bottom door, quietly watching the mom and baby until the mare wandered over. Nate placed a carrot chunk in the palm of his hand and held it out to the mare, her soft muzzle grazing his palm. Once she'd taken it, he opened the door, and walked in, motioning for Josh to follow him.

"Hey pretty lady. How are you doing?" Nate crooned softly and moved slowly. He hung his bag on a hook by the door and retrieved a thermometer and stethoscope. He looped the stethoscope around his neck. "I just need to make sure everything is still fine."

He clipped a lead line to the horse's halter and handed the line to Josh who quietly moved to the horse's head. Nate rested one hand on the horse's back, and placed the stethoscope against the horse's heart, checking his watch as he listened. Next he stood to the side and watched her sides move in and out as he timed her respirations.

The foal nudged Nate as it tried to get to the teat. "Just a minute, little one." Nate gently deflected the foal from its intended target. "I need to check your mom's udder and milk flow before you have at it again." He knelt down in the straw and proceeded with his exam. Satisfied that all was well, he turned his attention to the foal.

Josh knew the drill. He knelt down and securely hugged the skittish baby to his chest. Nate checked the foals' vital signs then took a blood sample. When they moved back into the barn aisle, Nate sat on a bench, pulled out his PC tablet and entered his notes. Done, Nate slipped it in his bag and leaned against the wall.

"What's the deal? Why would Cindy want sole custody? You're a great dad and have been nothing but fair considering what she did." It made him uncomfortable to roam into personal territory, but the elephant in the room wasn't going away. His mouth quirked in a rueful grin. He didn't miss the irony. Here he was getting his brother to talk about *his* elephant while he ignored his own.

"It's OK, you can say it. She cheated on me." Josh leaned forward and rested his hands on his knees. "She's making noises about taking a job in California next year when the divorce is final. Joint custody might put a crimp in her plans."

"Wow." Nate put his hand on Josh's back and leaned close. "You know your family's got your back? Right?"

"Yeah, I do. That's what's getting me through this."

"What would you do if she got permission to take Chad out of state?" Nate understood what it meant to have people you loved ripped from you and didn't envy Josh's position.

"Fight with everything I've got? Follow her? I don't know." Josh tipped his head back and studied the ceiling. "I only know I want to do what's best for Chad. A four-year-old shouldn't have to be in the middle of this."

Nate slapped his brother's knee. They were both silent for a moment, each lost in his own thoughts.

"So is Lauren the reason you're seeing a little light at the end of the tunnel?"

"Maybe," Nate's tone cautious. Probably whispered in his ear causing his body to contract like a turtle back into its shell. He wasn't supposed to feel anything for her but he did.

"Come on. Fess up, bro. I saw the way you looked at her at the playoff game."

If he wanted to get his family off his back, he had to make them believe he and Lauren were a couple. "I'm attracted to her for sure. Don't know yet whether we're suited for long-term." He hung his head. "We're a pair. Love doesn't seem to be in the cards for us."

"Beginning to look that way, but you've got a shot at it. Don't blow it." Josh stood up. "I've got to go. I promised Chad I'd take him to MacDonald's for dinner, and sounds like you've got work to do."

"Yup, miles to go before I sleep. You take care."

"You too. Mom's been nagging me to be on hand by Friday to set up for the rodeo. I assume, I'll see you then?"

"If any of us *don't* show up, we better be dead or mom will make us wish we were."

"Amen to that, brother."

Even without his mother's demand, he'd be at his parent's ranch this weekend. He was looking forward to seeing Lauren. That had to be a good sign. He didn't need a counselor poking around in his head. Nate headed to the next stall, his step a little lighter at the thought he could handle things on his own.

****

The receptionist buzzed to say Lauren's next client was here. She looked forward to seeing Todd. He seemed much happier now that he'd started going to the LGBT teen youth group and the school had added additional anti-bullying awareness sessions for students and teachers.

"Hey buddy," she said as she greeted him.

He grinned up at her.

"I love seeing that smile." She shoulder-bumped him and

led the way back to her office. She opted to sit on the small sofa with him instead of separate overstuffed chairs. She wanted him to feel accepted and comfortable with their growing bond.

He picked up the bottle of apple juice that was already waiting for him. He lifted it in salute. "Thanks."

"You seem happier. Tell me about the youth group. How's it going?" The sullen, depressed youth was gradually fading. Lauren could see a very different life for him on the horizon.

"Good. I've been going every Tuesday night. Met some people I like."

"How does that make you feel?" Did a shadow cross his face? She couldn't be sure. Teens were good at hiding their true feelings.

"Not so alone. I volunteered to work with some of the younger kids this summer and also spend more time at the animal shelter. I've always wanted a dog." He looked so hopeful, it made Lauren's heart swell.

"And your parents? Are things better with them?"

"Better. Mom's gone to a couple of parent meetings." He shrugged. "They're making an effort."

"And school?"

"Bullying's not so bad anymore, but I still get weird looks from people."

"How do you interpret that reaction?" Definite shadow. Todd was holding something back. She'd have to make a point of getting to the bottom of it in future sessions.

"Like I'm some sort of bad person. I hate that. Always wondering if someone is going to hurt me. Can't wait for school to let out."

"Fair enough. Let's talk about the videos you watched and what you've learned from your journaling…"

****

"Thanks for seeing me," said Josh, the shy Kincaid sibling,

sitting across from Lauren in her office.

While he had the same 'handsome' gene as his brothers, there were marked differences. He wore a baseball cap instead of a Stetson, sneakers instead of boots, his hair stylishly shaggy. He was much more the computer nerd than the cowboy.

"I'm happy I can to help." Divorce was tough, but Josh had extra hurdles in his path. No one in his immediate family was divorced—he'd be the first—and he was extremely shy. He rather be anywhere but in the spotlight. Lauren would need to be extra sensitive as she probed for answers. "You wanted to talk about concerns you have about Chad. Is that right?" She glanced at her notes. "He's four, correct?"

"Yeah, still a baby really. I'm worried about him."

"What makes you think Chad might be having problems?"

"He's changed since Cindy and I separated. He's clingier and he's carrying around his old teddy bear again, even at preschool. He goes ballistic if he can't find it. He's not the same little boy he was eight months ago. It's breaking my heart."

"I'm so sorry." She put her hand over his and her spirits sagged like an overladen bookshelf. She wished with all her heart she could make his problems go away. "Other than your separation, has anything changed in his relationship with you or Cindy?" Josh was smart and kind and considerate. Why was it certain women couldn't appreciate what they had?

Josh stood and started pacing as he spoke. "She met a guy right after we split—at least she says she only met him afterwards but who knows. He's a CEO at a tech company in California. That's why she's thinking about looking for a job there." He lifted his baseball cap and scrubbed his hand over his hair. "We've been arguing about it and Chad must have heard."

"Children naturally pick up on tension between their parents. You're their lifeline after all. Any chance you and

Cindy can talk when Chad isn't around? Maybe before he's picked up from daycare?"

Josh sank back down on the chair, elbows propped on knees, his head in his hands. "We've pretty much said everything that can be said on the subject. Now we're at a stalemate. The arguing has stopped, but Cindy resents not getting her way. I'm afraid some of that might be spilling over into what Chad hears when he's with her."

"Have you talked to her about your concerns over Chad?" She put her pen down on her pad and studied him mulling over how to phrase the next question. "Do you suspect Cindy might be trying to turn him against you? That she might not have Chad's best interests at heart?"

"No. God, no." He straightened up. "She may always be reaching for that next bigger gold ring, but she loves Chad. She wouldn't intentionally do anything to hurt him." He smiled but it didn't reach his eyes. "Hurt me, I'd believe. Honestly, though, I doubt she thinks I'm worth the bother. I was just one more step along her path."

Lauren picked up her pen and scribbled a note. "Then let's make sure Chad doesn't get hurt in the crossfire."

"I'll do anything to protect my son." His eyes narrowed and a muscle ticked along his jaw.

"Understood. At the end of this session I'll give you some information to share with Cindy on helping Chad deal with the changes he's experiencing. I'll also give you age-appropriate books to read with him to help initiate a conversation about what he's feeling. Right now though, I'd like to focus on you and how you're coping."

At the end of the session, Lauren ushered Josh to the client exit. She put a hand on his arm as he reached for the door. "I want you to know, no matter what happens with Nate and me, please consider me your friend. I hope you'll come to me whenever you need someone to talk to."

He leaned down and gave her a shy hug. "Thanks. I appreciate it. You and Ashley are like the sisters I never had." With a final awkward pat on the back, he left.

****

She closed the door, walked to the middle of the room, and sat down on the floor cross-legged. Shutting her eyes she performed a yoga 'om,' then went in search of Jasmine. She found her at her desk catching up on paperwork. Lauren sank gracefully into a chair across from her.

"I need some decompression time before my next client."

Jasmine pushed the papers to the side and hands folded together, rested her forearms on the desk. "Rough one?"

"I hate divorce cases. The part of me that believes in happily-ever-after is deeply offended." She lifted the end metal ball on the kinetic sculpture on Jasmine's desk and dropped it, setting the other balls in motion.

"You and I both know happy endings aren't always possible." Jasmine captured the line of balls in her hand silencing them. "What's really bothering you?" She sat back in her chair and waited.

"It's hard enough to counsel clients I don't know and not be affected by their pain. When it's someone I know…" Lauren looked down at the fingers she was drumming on her thighs and willed them to be still. "Josh is such a sweet guy and doesn't deserve this. Not that anyone does." Her words tumbled out. "I know we need to keep professional distance with our clients, but this is Josh. He's so shy. I know he wouldn't open up to someone else like he does with me so I'm the one who needs to see him."

"You can't heal the world. There will always be clients or situations you can't fix." Jasmine used her fingertips to roll a pen back and forth on her desk, but her gaze was direct. "We've talked about this. Getting too involved emotionally—plus over confidence that you can fix everyone—can come back to bite you in the butt."

Lauren ran a finger across her forehead brushing a strand of hair out of her face, and nodded slowly. "I'm working on lowering my expectations, but I'm positive I can help if my patients will only follow my advice."

"Part of being a good psychologist is the belief we make a positive impact on people's lives, but we also need to balance that with a healthy dose of reality. Just remember, when you start getting sucked in, talk to someone.

CHAPTER TEN

Nate heard the undercurrent of sexual interest rippling across the barnyard and looked up from combing his horse's mane to see what was causing the stir. And there it was, the definition of sexy striding toward the bleachers. Lauren and Ashley were chatting and laughing oblivious to the wishful looks from the men.

All week his heart pranced like a colt when he thought about seeing her. He texted her a few times – silly things, like he thought of her and picked something healthy for lunch, and he'd heard a song they'd danced to. He even called once simply to hear her voice. He'd had to put down his parent's dog, the one he'd played with as a child. Her compassion and patience as she listened to him, made him feel better. He'd never acted this way around Sharon. A lump the size of a watermelon sat in his chest. This wasn't serious, it was about keeping up appearances. She'd have something to show her friends to prove they were a couple. His ploy seemed to be working because his family had eased up on him lately.

Lauren glanced his way, smiled the smile that made his heart stop, and shifted course toward him. Ashley peeled off in Zach's direction. Long strides brought Lauren closer and closer. What that woman did to a pair of jeans. Tight. Tantalizing. Tempting as sin. No wonder all those big name brands wanted her to model for them. A tank top hugged her breasts and scooped just low enough to give a man a glimpse of paradise. The flannel shirt, casually knotted at her waist, and jean jacket said sweet, but the rest of the package said hot with a capital 'H.'

"Hi there, stud. I hear you know how to show a girl a

good time." Her low, sultry voice rocketed into his ear like a torpedo, sending shockwaves throughout his body. She walked her fingers up his chest. "Hello in there. What's the matter? Can't speak?"

He nodded and cleared his throat. She could tease a smile out of him and lighten his spirits like no one else. "Glad you could make it." He couldn't think straight when she was around. Couldn't recall the fear that dogged him. Wistfulness for what could be if they actually were a couple nibbled around the edges.

She stepped back and examined him slowly. "I've never seen you in cowboy duds." She rubbed a bit of his sleeve between her fingers. "What is it about a cowboy that makes a woman go weak in the knees?"

"I don't know, but I hope it rubs off on me." The image of her collapsing into his arms made him go weak in the knees.

Lauren gave him three quick pats to the cheek. "It's beneath you to fish for compliments. I see how women look at you. Lascivious images dancing in their heads."

He ran his hands up her arms, "Is that how you see me? Lascivious images?" His lips were close to her ear and she leaned into him as they brushed against her tender lobe.

She didn't say a word, just melted into him. He wrapped his arms around her, rested his chin on the top of her head, and held her for a minute. She felt good in his arms. He realized he hadn't felt the usual kick of fear when he started wanting her. Maybe he *could* love again. Nothing wrong with him. He was fine. Or, a sarcastic voice whispered, maybe it simply depended which part of his body he was thinking with.

Nate, told the sarcastic voice to shut up and stepped back, holding her at arm's length so he could look in her eyes. "I'm going to have to head into the arena soon. I'll be kept hopping until lunch, but after that, I'm all yours." He kissed her again, telling himself he needed to put on a good performance. He could tell himself whatever he wanted, but he knew it was because it felt good. "Will you be staying for the dance?"

"Some of it. It's tax season and Ashely has to work tomorrow so we need to leave early. Save a few dances for me?"

"All of them, honey. All of them." He turned her around and gave her a gentle push and pat on the seat of her pants. "See you by the lunch truck at noon." Nate placed his hand over his heart, his gaze zeroing in on her delectable backside as she walked toward the stands.

****

Crystal waved and patted the seat beside her. "I saved a spot for you and Ashley," she hollered. They hugged when Lauren reached her.

"Looks like Ashley will be a bit delayed," Crystal said nodding in the direction of Ashley and Zach who were twined around each other like wisteria.

Ashley reached them as the riders swept into the arena. A lump formed in Lauren's throat as she watched them gallop in front of the stands, each carrying an American flag whipping in the wind behind them. The sight got her every time. When the crowd sang the National Anthem and recited the Pledge of Allegiance, she turned into a puddle of patriotic emotion. Respect, courtesy, and friendship hadn't gone out of style in the rodeo world. You didn't walk by someone you knew without asking how they were doing—and actually being interested in the answer. Much as she loved her family and South Carolina, this is where she belonged.

Nate looked so manly on his horse, easily calming it as it tossed its head ready to go. She'd never seen Nate compete, but would be surprised if he didn't give his rodeo champion brother a run for his money. Turned out when the team roping event came up, Nate and Wayne came in a close second. Naturally Zach and his partner, Matt, took top honors but hey, that's what they did for a living.

Lauren popped up as the last event before lunch ended. "Okay ladies, lunchtime." She rubbed her hands together. "Don't want to be the last in line. Let's get moving." Nate was waiting for her and a zing of excitement shot through her like a triple expresso.

Crystal put her hand on Lauren's arm. "Sweetie, they aren't going to run out of food. What's your rush?"

"I think it has something to do with a certain veterinarian." Ashley slapped Lauren on the back. "Come on pal, I'm with you. Two hot guys waiting for us does make a lady wanna be quick out of the chute."

The two wormed their way through the crush of people heading for the food trucks. Lauren turned when Ashely suddenly disappeared around the corner of one of the barns. When she saw that it was Zach who had nabbed her friend, she waved and made a beeline for Nate. The man was hard to miss, taller than any of the men around him.

She came up behind him, slipped her arms around his middle and rested her cheek against his broad back. It was nice having a man who was taller than her. Made her feel all feminine.

"I was beginning to wonder where you were." He tugged on her arm, tucking her against his side, his arm across her shoulders. "I was just about to come looking for you." He let his lips brush her temple and he stepped away from the people he'd been talking too.

"Hungry? I promise these will rank among the best fish and carne asada tacos you'll ever eat. And the salsa…" He brought his fingertips to his lips, kissed them, and swept his hand heavenward. "To die for."

"It smells wonderful." She tucked her arm through his as they settled at a table. He played the boyfriend part well— holding her chair for her, casual touches, feeding her a bite of his taco, and dabbing the corner of her lips with a napkin. The way he looked at her made her wish this wasn't pretend.

After they'd eaten, Lauren licked her fingers, noticed Nate watching so took her time, giving each finger the attention it deserved. When beads of perspiration dotted his forehead, she grinned and sat back in the folding wooden chair. With her hands on her stomach she said, "That was good. Better than good actually. I am officially stuffed. I don't suppose a nap is next on the agenda?"

Nate brushed a wisp of hair from her face. She leaned into his touch. "Honey, if we find ourselves horizontal together, napping will be the last thing on my mind." His husky voice skittered along her nerve endings and skidded into desire, hot and ready. Yeah, napping would so *not* happen.

"I was going to check on the animals. Can I talk you into joining me?"

She nodded her head. "Anything involving getting up and moving sounds like a plan."

****

He took her hand and they strolled to one of the smaller barns. They entered stuck together like two pieces of polyester fresh out of the dryer, crackling with electricity. The laughter and squeals of small children, drew them to the far end. They found Josh leaning on the railing of a pen while six preschoolers chased an equal number of baby goats.

Lauren pulled her phone out of her pocket and started recording. "This is too cute for words." She stepped up on the bottom rail, then the second rail, and was soon in the pen in the middle of the mayhem. The sight of her surrounded by children thrummed deep in Nate's chest pulling longing closer to the surface. She dazzled no matter where she was and the sparkle seemed to be rubbing off on him.

Moving to stand next to his brother, he sensed his unhappiness. Nate wished some of Lauren's sparkle could rub off on Josh too.

"I see you have Chad today. How's he doing splitting his time between you and Cindy?"

"He was never much of a crier before. Now he cries

when I pick him up because he wants his mommy, and when I drop him off cries because he wants to stay with me. It's like I'm in a carnival funhouse and don't know which way is out."

"Seems to be having fun today with all his cousins. That's something."

"It's one of the arguments I plan to make against Cindy getting sole custody. He has so much family here and he's close to them."

"Cindy's still talking about moving?"

"Yeah, she is... Look, I'm up for saddle bronc riding. Can you watch Chad for a little while?"

"Of course, but don't you want us to bring Chad to the stands to watch your event?"

"No it will be over in seconds and right now he's having so much fun with his cousins. Besides, I don't want him to watch me get bucked off a horse and worry about me getting hurt."

"Got it." Nate clapped his brother on the back.

Josh straightened and strode out of the barn. Nate's phone rang and he reached for it out of habit, not focused on the call, but on the woman playing with the children.

"This is Nate... Hey, Sue Ann." He listened for a moment. "Thanks for letting me know, but it sounds like you have everything under control. No need for me to check... Talk to you later." He paused as he started to slip the phone back in its clip, revelation sneaking up on him. He had absolutely no desire to dash off and oversee the work Sue Ann was doing. Hmm, maybe he could let go of some things.

Nate propped his elbows on the top rail and rested his chin on his hands, a lopsided grin on his face. Lauren was good with the kids. Someday she'd make a great mom. One little girl had crawled into her lap and was being rocked while rambunctious children cavorted around her throwing straw in the air. Bits of it caught in Lauren's hair. Her delight, floating in the air like dust moats, enveloped his heart. Warm. Welcoming. Wanted.

She turned her head and beamed up at him. Contentment sat by his side like an old friend, something he hadn't felt around a woman in a good, long while. One of the baby goats scampered by, crashing into her arm as it dodged several of the boys' attempts to corral it. Her deep belly laugh pulled him into the pen to join her. Nate chased the youngsters, tickling them when he caught them. Their squeals set the sheep in the next pen to bleating.

"Kids, I think it's time to leave the animals alone," Nate said. At their protests, he crossed his arms and used the steely-eyed glare that had always worked on his brothers and younger cousins. The little ones quietly filed out of the pen. Good to know he hadn't lost his touch. Nate waved as Josh approached. "How'd you do?"

"Held my own and didn't break anything. That's a win in my book. Since I spend a lot more time sitting in front of a computer than I do on a bucking horse, I'm happy to be in one piece." Josh caught his son who had charged toward him and swung him around, letting his feet fly out behind him. "Closing ceremony is coming up so we've got to saddle our horses and get ready." Josh ruffled his son's hair. "Come on squirt and help your dad."

Nate and Lauren followed them to the main barn where Nate led his big bay gelding out of the stall. He tethered it to a ring in the wall and handed Lauren a finishing brush. "Know what to do with one of these?"

"Sure do."

"Good, just a light brushing before I saddle him up." Nate picked up the mane and tail brush and got to work. "Would you like to meet me at the barbeque after the finale or would you rather hang out with Ashely until the dancing starts?"

Lauren glanced over at Ashley and Zack who were obviously hot for each other. "I don't think she's going to be available. Guess you're stuck with me."

"My lucky day, then." It surprised him that he believed what he said.

CHAPTER ELEVEN

Lauren wrapped one, long blonde strand around the curling iron, then another and another until a waterfall of curls tumbled down her back. Nate had promised to call after the rodeo and—surprise, surprise—he had. He'd given her a choice between a basketball game or a club with a jazz combo. So sweet of him to let her decide. She'd surprised him by choosing basketball. Didn't want him to think he had her figured out.

She perused her box of side combs and barrettes, finally selecting a pair of Swarovski crystal combs to pull her hair away from her face. She dabbed Kate Spade *Walk on Air* perfume behind her ears and at the pulse. Oh why not, she thought and pulled up her silky top to dab the light floral mix between her breasts. Who knows, he might get close enough to smell it.

Her heart tapped to the beat of an Irish jig when the doorbell sounded. She grabbed her velvet jacket, a merino wool scarf, and her purse off the bed on her way to answer the door. She closed her eyes and took a deep, cleansing breath before pulling it open.

And there he stood, all six foot five glorious inches of delectable hunk, hat in his hand, rotating it counter clockwise. Nervous? Scared? Her mouth went dry at the sight of him and a tender bubble popped in her chest coating her with its buoyant film. All she wanted to do was to put him at ease and a smile in his heart.

After helping her into her jacket, he bent and kissed her nape, turned her to face him, and ran his hands down her arms. "I like your jacket. It's soft." The sensations he evoked made her want to skip the date and stay home by the fire, but there was something to be said for anticipation.

She touched his lips with hers then placed her hand against his broad chest. "I'm glad I chose the Spurs game over the jazz combo. My mood tonight is more cheering and energy, than laid-back and mellow," Lauren said.

"I'm glad you chose the Spurs too. I added the jazz option because you didn't seem caught up in the football playoff game. I wasn't sure sports were your thing." He opened the door to his truck and helped her in.

"I like sports fine," she said as they pulled out of the driveway. "Football's not my favorite, but please don't tell anyone or I'll be blackballed from the sisterhood of Southern women."

"You can probably buy my silence."

His grin made her breath catch in her throat and bathed her body in heat. "And just what might it take to keep my reputation in tact?" She had a couple of ideas – one involved whipped cream – but she was curious what he would come up with.

"Skinny dipping on a hot summer day would be nice, but since its February, would you consider sitting on a sofa in front of a fire keeping each other warm?"

"Any chance whipped cream is involved in your fantasy?"

"Huh?"

"Never mind. You, me, together on the sofa. That works." She patted his arm when she saw the light bulb go off and his eyebrows shoot up. She wondered if underneath his traditional persona was a red hot lover. Imagining what kind of lover he might be, made her nipples tighten. She swallowed hard.

Watching him smile, the easy banter, having him join her in singing the chorus to a song on the radio, had her mood soaring like a hot air balloon in the still morning. The more he loosened up, the greater the likelihood he'd be willing to take risks again. She wanted to be one of those risks. As they pulled up to the arena, she reached over the console and touched his hand. "This is beginning to feel like a real date."

He shifted his hand out from under hers and turned to pay the parking attendant. "Let's not get ahead of ourselves. What's wrong with what we have right now? Enjoying each other's company. No complications." A muscle along his jaw ticked.

"Why would actually dating me be a complication?" Her hot air balloon crashed and burst into flames in a field of weeds.

"Because if this weren't pretend, we would have reached my four date limit. After that, women start wanting things I'm not willing to give." He parked the car and looked at her with suspicion in his eyes. "You aren't getting serious on me are you?"

"No. Like you, I don't have time for serious right now." Lies were proliferating in her world like ants on a crumb. She was lying to herself and lying to him. She let him take her hand, but the easy camaraderie had evaporated.

****

Nate went to fetch food while Lauren watched the teams warm up. He glanced up at one of the overhead televisions while he waited in line. His jaw dropped, his heart stilled. There was Lauren, draped in a skin-tight gown, moving gracefully, confidently across a room filled with equally glamorous people, but she glowed like a lighthouse, shining so much brighter than anything around her. The perfume company sponsoring the commercial was getting its money's worth. He'd buy a bottle, maybe a thousand.

He wasn't the only man thinking that thought. Two guys behind him were discussing her physical attributes in excruciating detail and what they'd like to do with those attributes. His hands balled into fists. He had to clamp down tightly on the urge to plant his fists squarely on the jaws of those two idiots. While those same fantasies ran like a movie reel in his head too—though he'd perform them with much more finesse and care—the thought of another man with his hands on Lauren tightened him like a panther ready to spring. Luckily the clerk asked for his order before he did anything stupid.

Burgers, fries, and beers in hand, he walked back to their seats. Before moving across the row, he paused to soak in the sight of her. She leaned forward, elbows resting on her knees, following the action on the court, chatting amiably with the couple next to her, laughing, clapping, in the moment. She brought light to darkness and confidence to uncertainty. Shit. Why had he behaved so badly when she suggested this felt like a real date? She turned and waved him in with a smile. Had he imagined her annoyance in the parking lot or did this mean it didn't matter to her one way or the other if they were a couple or not? His heart clenched and he mentally shook himself. They weren't a couple. End of story.

"Miss me?" he asked once he'd shuffled over to her. They weren't a real couple but he had to put on a show.

"Sure did," she gave him a quick peck on the cheek, "especially since I knew you were out foraging for sustenance." She wiggled her fingers. "Gimme. Gimme."

He puckered his lips and raised his eyebrows. He couldn't believe he was angling for a kiss in front of all these people. Lauren did that to a man—tossed a sense of restraint on its keister.

"You drive a hard bargain, mister." She laced her fingers behind his head and dove in for a deep, satisfying, toe curling kiss that left them both breathless and had the people around them clapping. "Can I have my food now?" Her voice breathed spring into his winter soul.

He silently passed her a basket of burger and fries, and a glass of beer. "You're not annoyed with me?"

"What's the point? If I stay mad, that'll ruin my evening. I choose to relax and enjoy whatever time we have together."

Maybe he should take a cue from her. Relax and enjoy.

Lights dimmed, players images flashed on the jumbotron, cheering escalated, and the announcer shouted the starting lineup. Everyone stood for the National Anthem and the game began. Three hours of noise, action, emotional ups and downs, lots of hugging and hand-wringing later, the Spurs emerged victorious.

"Now that was a game for the ages. Wow," Lauren said. She gave him a high-five on their way to his truck.

"I was expecting a good game, but this..." He made fists in front of his body and pulled downward. "We're going to be telling our grandkids we were at this game." Did he just say, 'our grandkids'? And the earth hadn't opened and swallowed him whole? A hint of guilt seeped in. Sharon had been his everything once. Was he disrespecting her memory?

Her happy dance brought a smile to his lips. The jiggly parts jiggled nicely, and the rest, well a man would have to be blind or dead if he wasn't captivated by the motion. Her joie de vivre was contagious. When he was with her, his world seemed as fresh and clean as the morning after a rain.

They climbed into his truck and he looked at the long line of vehicles waiting to exit the parking lot. "Looks like we have a few minutes to kill." Lucky him.

He leaned across the console slowly, wanting to give her time to move away in case he'd misread the signals. Brushing his hand along her jaw, closing the distance between them inch by agonizing inch, hunger for her growled in his belly. Her breath shimmered against his cheek, he could smell the chocolate she'd eaten earlier, began to taste it as their lips merged. He kissed the corner of her mouth and hers open, inviting him to deepen the kiss. He thought his heart would explode. He teased the tip of her tongue with his. He wanted the kiss to go on, but it was definitely time to get out of the parking lot. Stunned, he realized he'd kissed her with abandon, without fear, and something deep inside him shifted.

****

Barking dogs greeted them at her door which they promptly shooed outside. He didn't say anything, words weren't necessary, just took her hand and led her into the living room, to the sofa. Cradling her face in his hands, he marveled at the softness. He slipped her jacket down her arms, his rough hands catching on her silky top, and shrugged out of his own. With a flick of the wrist, he tossed them aside not caring where they landed. He sat and pulled off his boots then stood in front of her again.

Lips slid over each other like otters frolicking in the snow. Pure joy at being alive. His hands traveled down her ribs, learning her feminine curves before shifting to the base of her spine, melding her to him. He wasn't sure how they got there, but they were soon prone on the sofa, her back cradled by the back cushions, he on the edge both literally and figuratively. He nipped the hollow in her throat softly with his lips, cupped her full breasts in his hands, and teased her nipples with his thumbs through the silky fabric of her top. He felt the rosy buds pebble under his touch.

She placed her hands against his chest, easing him back so she could grab the hem of her top and pull it over her head. He reached around and unfastened her bra and stared for a moment at the wonder of her. He kissed the top of one creamy mound, continuing to the nipple, taking it in his mouth, worshiping her with his tongue. The other breast received the same adoration. Her silken hair tangled in his fists. Her hands traced down his back driving him mad.

"I want to feel your skin next to mine," Lauren whispered.

Her request parked what rational thought he had left on a moon on the far side of the galaxy. He eased back enough to undo the buttons of his shirt without falling off the sofa. Her busy fingers helped speed the process along, searing him through his t-shirt wherever they touched. He rotated to a sitting position to shrug out of his shirt and pull his t-shirt over his head. She leaned forward and kissed the indent at his lower back. Fire shot up his spine and he thought he might need a defibrillator. When he lay back down, she rubbed her breasts against his now exposed skin. Was spontaneous combustion a possibility?

Ringing. He heard ringing and something vibrated against his hip. Maybe he'd died and gone to heaven and the bells were pealing? Shit. His phone. His office ringtone. It wasn't his night to be on call. Why was it ringing? Could he ignore it? No, never. Work always came first. It had to. Too much rode on the success of the business. There must be an emergency. He rolled to a sitting position, pulling the phone out of his belt clip with one hand and sliding a hand down her hair with the other. Regret in his gesture, in his voice.

"I have to take this. It's my office." His tone now brisk, "Nate here." He listened for a minute. "It sounds like I'll need to do surgery. Have him meet me at the clinic in 20 minutes."

He shifted to look down at her. "I have to go. Two of the three vets in our practice are out on calls. Looks like every horse in the county decided to have an emergency tonight." He leaned over and kissed her lips, sighed deeply, and kissed each breast.

"Do you really have to go? Can't your third partner take this one?"

"No. I'm next in rotation. I have to go." His voice sounded glacial. He had to push her away. He couldn't let her interfere with his work. He couldn't give in to what he wanted to do which was climb back on the sofa with Lauren. Leaving her warmth was one of the hardest things he'd ever done. She sat up, serene and beautiful. Swinging her long legs to the floor, she stood up and helped him button his shirt, kissing him longingly on the lips and down to the hollow of his throat and he groaned. He saw the hurt in her eyes. His resolve waivered, but didn't buckle. The trapped feeling returned. He couldn't give her what he suspected she was beginning to want.

Despite the kick of fear, his arms went around her and he kissed her one more time, to take the sweetness of her with him. He sat and pulled on his boots then stood, looked around, found his jacket and shrugged into it. He put on his hat and was out the door. Don't look back the tormentor in his head said or he might not be able to leave. The fear clawed at his gut again. Caring too much had crippled him before. He couldn't be pulled back into the darkness again.

CHAPTER TWELVE

He'd called her and invited her to spend a day at his ranch to make up for the other night. His two Australian Cattle dogs, Aussie and Clyde, herded Lauren's CRV to a parking spot on Nate's driveway. Their job done, they flopped down in the shade of the portico waiting for their next task.

The trusty German Shephard never left his master's side and calmly watched the antics of the other dogs. Nate, leaning against the barn opening, absently scratched Bear's ears. Her car door opened and his feet started moving. It had only been a few days since he'd seen her but anticipation danced in his gut, the sky seemed bluer, and the air lighter. He'd been worrying about his dad's upcoming surgery. Hated returning to the hospital where his first love had slipped slowly, painfully, from this world. Letting it gnaw at him like lions tearing apart their catch. Worst case scenarios pummeling his brain. Seeing Lauren shoved everything off to the side of the railroad tracks, at least for a while.

His strides lengthened as desire and longing thrummed along every nerve in his body. When he reached her, he grabbed her in a hug and swung her around lifting her feet from the ground. She put her hand on her hat to keep it in place as he twirled her in a circle.

Her laughter and joy tapped a hidden spring of happiness he hadn't drunk from in far too long. While he hadn't been exactly dour since Sharon's death, he hadn't felt this well of pure pleasure surging like a geyser from a source buried deep below the surface.

Once her feet touched the ground, she looked up at his

house. "Nice place, but doesn't look like you."

"Someone built it for speculation when the market was hot. When it crashed, I picked it up cheap." He stood back trying to see it through her eyes. The builder had designed the house to appeal to the nouveau riche, gentleman rancher type. It could just as easily have been placed in an upscale Dallas neighborhood instead of 40 acres outside San Antonio.

"If I'd built it from scratch, it would look a lot less pretentious." He held his hand up to frame the view. "Probably some river rock on the exterior, wood beams, peaked roof lines. Definitely not this, but it'll make a great family home someday."

"You see a wife and children in your future?"

"Of course. I've always wanted a family." He did want a family. It was the wife part that caused him grief. The first without the second wasn't going to happen. Why couldn't Lauren be the kind of woman who didn't make him feel?

"We all have our dreams," Lauren said. "They're what make life worth living." She cocked her head and examined the house. "If you didn't like the house, why buy it? Surely there were other properties available."

"I fell in love with the land. There was enough flat property fronting the main road to build my clinic and the house was far enough away I don't feel like I'm living at work. You ready for our trail ride?"

Impulsively, he bent her back over his arm and swooped in for a kiss. When the bells started ringing, his heart started racing, and fear nibbled at his subconscious, he decided it was time to hit the pause button. Why couldn't being with her be easy? "The horses are saddled and waiting. Shame to waste this nice weather. Can you stay for lunch? I picked up a piece of salmon to grill and have fresh fruits and vegetables. Even bought some of that humus you like."

"Honey, you had me at the kiss." He hooked her arm in his and headed for the barn.

****

Nate relaxed into the warmth of the mild spring sun, the soothing rhythm of the horse's gait, the scent of earth and vegetation filling his nostrils, and birds flittering between the trees. Perfect.

"I'd forgotten how totally at peace I am when I'm on the back of a horse," Lauren said. "I feel like I'm one with nature. Weird, huh?"

"Nope. Every horse person knows exactly what you mean." He nudged his big bay gelding forward to see what the two Australian Cattle dogs were making a fuss over. He heard the distinct bawling of a calf. Calling the dogs back, Nate dismounted, and climbed into a shallow ravine.

"What are you doing out here away from the herd?" He talked quietly and approached slowly. Kneeling down, he performed a quick physical inspection of the calf and its mama. "Looks like you're both doing fine. What's the matter mama? You wanted some privacy to have your calf? I think it's time to get you back in the pasture and then figure out how you escaped."

Nate hoisted the calf in his arms, climbed out of the ravine, and settled the calf across his saddle. From the look in Lauren's greedy eyes, she was duly impressed with his prowess. The two herding dogs made sure mama followed. He remounted, carefully positioning himself behind his noisy passenger.

"I've been working with Zach to breed Corriente cattle. They're sturdy, but tend to be escape artists so I have to keep an eye on them. I also have a herd of angora goats."

"Angora goats? I love working with mohair." In response to his quizzical look. "I knit." She fingered the infinity scarf hanging from her neck.

They rode on until they reached the gate. He released the calf and mama into the pasture.

"Won't they get out again?" Lauren asked.

"I'm leaving Aussie and Clyde here until I've patched the

fence. They'll keep them in line." He motioned the dogs inside and they smoothly herded the mama and calf back to the other cattle before belly flopping onto the turf, alert and ready to work.

"Would you like to see the goats?"

"Very much." She turned her horse to follow Nate back down the trail. Shifting slightly in the saddle, Lauren rubbed her thigh. "I'd forgotten the workout your leg muscles get when you ride. I'll have to do more of this."

"Have you ridden much before?"

"Up until I went away to college, all the time. My family boarded our horses in a community stable and the area is crisscrossed with riding trails. I also spent a lot of time on Ashley's plantation where our main source of transportation was by horseback."

"Funny, I always pictured you as a city girl."

"Nope, I'm country all the way. Charleston is not exactly a metropolis and we lived outside town. In 4-H Ashley and I raised angora goats and she eventually added a herd to her plantation livestock."

"Wait a minute. What's the name of her plantation?" Nate asked.

"Charlotte's Creek."

"Small world. I bought my breeding stock from them. Dealt with someone named…" He scratched his head. "Michael."

"That's Ashley's brother." She twisted in the saddle to face him. "*I can't wait to tell her some of her goats are right here in San Antonio.*"

They rounded a bend and the vista opened to a broad meadow dotted with live oak, maple, cedar, and mesquite trees. Wildflowers and wild grasses carpeted the field. Several lean-tos were scattered around to provide shelter for the animals during the cool nights and occasional rain.

A large herd of nanny goats grazed peacefully while their kids frolicked. "You can see that kidding season is in full swing. They look pretty good right now compared to the matted mess they were before we sheered them last month."

"I don't know how you do it. A busy veterinary practice and yet, here you are, adding herds of goats and cattle to your workload." Her lips curved softly. "You are one crazy dude."

He rested both hands on the saddle horn, relaxed, enjoying the scene. "I like staying busy and experiment with new things." He pushed his hat back on his head and looked over at her. "Something else I inherited from my grandpa."

"I haven't met any of your grandparents. Are they still in the area?"

"They all passed away within a year when I was 12. Rough year." He looked down at the ground, his sadness opened like a deep gorge, wild and untamed.

"I'm so sorry. Losing four people you love in such a short time must have been tough. What happened, if you don't mind my asking?"

"Grandpa Kincaid, the vet, had a heart attack when he was out on the range. We couldn't get him to the hospital quick enough." A vision of that day, his beloved grandpa clutching his chest and gasping for breath shivered down his arms in an army of menacing goosebumps. He'd felt so helpless. Could that be where his need for control came from?

"You were there?"

"Yeah," he sighed. The concern in her voice and the gentle touch of her fingers eased the ache that always settled in, like the first frost of fall. "Grandpa Hathaway had pancreatic cancer. I think both my grandmas just died of broken hearts. It was like they lost the will to live when their husband's passed."

"That's a lot for a young boy to take in." She paused as a thought struck her. "Do you think losing your grandparents like that might have affected the way you responded to your fiancé's death?"

He felt himself unfolding like an ocean wave in reverse, his spine straightening vertebra by vertebra. He rubbed his hand over the stubble on his chin. "I never thought about it in that light. It's possible a 12-year-old boy might not resolve emotional issues by himself." He'd have to ponder her observation a while before he knew what it meant.

"Talking to a therapist might help you figure it out."

Nate jerked the reins more forcefully than intended. "Sorry fella," he said patting the horse's neck. He'd pulled out the card she'd given him with Jasmine's number more than once. Each time he felt like he'd walked into a room full of lilies, their fragrance overwhelming and he had to get out into the fresh air. What if he went and discovered he was defective. He'd had his one shot at love and that's all he had to give. As though sensing his tension, his horse side-stepped and bounced its head. "Steady boy." Nate willed his body to relax.

"Let's get back. I'm getting hungry," Nate said. From the look on her face, he could tell she knew he was heavy into avoidance. He reined in his horse and she stopped beside him. "My Dad's going in for heart surgery next week." He had no idea why he blurted that out. Maybe to explain why he wasn't thinking straight.

"Oh my gosh. I'm sorry. Is it serious?"

"He's having a stent put in next week. The doctor says it's routine and dad's a great candidate." Nate swiped a sweaty palm on his jeans and hoped he could talk past the lump in his throat. "I'm probably blowing it out of proportion."

"Of course you're worried." Their legs bumped as the horses shifted. "One of my uncles had stent surgery. Once he'd recovered, it was hard to believe he was the same person. His life improved dramatically." She leaned over and squeezed his hand and Nate leaned into the comfort that small gesture brought. "It's only natural to be worried. Send me the details. I'd like to be with you at the hospital if it's alright with your family."

"Thanks. I will." He clucked his horse forward. "Saw one of your commercials the other day. Do you like modeling?" He knew he was avoiding talking in depth about uncomfortable subjects—and he knew she knew.

"I don't *dislike* it. The money's been good. I graduated from college without any debt. Not many can say that anymore."

"Amen to that one. I'm still paying off mine plus the cost of getting the clinic off the ground." Another worry that held his peace of mind in a choke hold. Debt everywhere he looked. The only thing between him and ruin, was the success of his practice.

"While counseling is where my heart's at, it's exciting to head off on a shoot. I have a location assignment in L.A. coming up next month."

"How long do your assignments usually last?"

"Generally a day or two plus travel, but since I have a brother and sister in L.A., I'm taking a few extra days for this trip." Lauren nudged her horse forward when it paused to snatch a mouthful of grass.

"If counseling is so important, why even bother modeling?"

"It's an added measure of security to make sure I can keep doing what I love. I'm still building my client list. The occasional modeling job means I don't have to worry about money and can concentrate on my clients."

They arrived in the stable yard. Nate dismounted and walked over to help her. She kicked her leg out of one stirrup and swung it over preparing to lower herself to the ground, but he was ready. The need to touch her irresistible. His hands spanned her waist and he crowded her so that she slipped down his body.

Nate turned her to face him, captured her face in his palms, and kissed her like she was the last jelly donut on the tray and he had to have it. Her body felt like warm butter, soft and pliant against him.

"I have to unsaddle the horses and turn them out to pasture, but don't go anywhere."

She sat on the bench and watched him work. He quickly removed the saddles, storing them on a rack in the tack room, replaced the bridals with halters, and turned their mounts lose in the pasture. He felt her watching him and he did his best to look strong and competent. Task complete his eyes lasered in on her lips. He held out his hands and she put hers into them. His hands moved to her back and pulled her tightly against him. His mouth moved to her throat and could feel her pulse beating beneath his lips. She arched back giving him access to the long column of her neck.

"What's say we take this inside?" he whispered.

She nodded. She warmed the cold place around his heart. The feelings scared him, but the warmth drew him forward.

CHAPTER THIRTEEN

Nate shut the front door, stopping in the entry. His hands smoothed up her arms imprinting the strength and caring of this man on her soul. Unbuttoning the top button of her shirt, he lowered his head, kissing the hollow of her throat, circling it slowly with his tongue. The emotions he unleashed tumbled and tossed like a twig in a tornado.

"I didn't invite you here today to make love to you, but it's what I want to do. If you're not okay with that, let me know now."

"Where's your bedroom?" Lauren couldn't think of anything she wanted more than to have this man inside her, filling her, being one with her. No more hesitancy in his touch. No holding back. No denying what he felt for her.

He planted one more soul-searing kiss on her lips, then her feet left the ground. Heavy steps on the stairs. Impressions. Dark, heavy furniture, masculine, a bed the size of a football field. He set her down beside the bed, the back of her knees touching the mattress.

Strong arms encircled her. His mouth teased down the column of her neck. Shivers of delight seized her as he lingered on the sensitive hollow beneath her ear, tasting her with the tip of his tongue. He turned what was a dam ready to overflow with passion into a controlled release, slowing the flood, letting them both savor the moment. Shaking fingers removed clothing, slowly, luxuriously. Sleeves skimmed down her arms, guided by calloused palms on soft skin. The shirt floated down to the floor like a feather off a tall building. He knelt, lowering the zipper of her jeans. Soft

105

kisses ringed her navel. Every touch celebrated her.

Sitting her on the bed with a gentle push, he pulled off her boots and socks, taking time to massage her feet. Magic hands worked their way up her legs. She arched back on her hands. So decadent. Teeth softly nipped her inner thigh through the fabric of her jeans. A purr reverberated deep in her chest. His hands slid under her butt and guided her to stand. Her abdomen rested against the silky softness of his hair. His hands slid down her hips, taking her jeans with them, leaving her in only her bra and panties. His mouth rained kisses down her thighs to her knees.

He stood up and moved back. It felt like he was drinking her in, absorbing her. Slowly he started unbuttoning his shirt, a strip tease just for her. Her butt hit the bed when her knees could no longer support her weight. Her mouth went dry. This was better than a birthday. Better than Christmas. The most amazing gift ever being unwrapped before her, layer by layer. Tantalizing. Breath-taking. Heart-pounding.

His shirt flipped through the air like a slow-motion Frisbee. His fingers lifted the hem of his t-shirt, provocatively, one rib at a time, revealing abs so ripped they made her want to weep, a sprinkling of blond hair that, like an arrow, dived below his waistband. No man boobs on these pectorals. The mouth that had been dry, turned moist and she had to swallow. Magnificent.

Nate moved to a leather recliner sitting in a corner of the massive room. No, her mind screamed and begged, don't move away. Her fingers itched to trace the outline of his chest, to feel the sinews beneath her fingers, and his hair tangled in her fists. He sat and pulled off his boots, all the time staring intently into her eyes. Locked on and loaded. She sizzled and craved.

The jeans were next. He stood, unbuttoning, then unzipping, letting the opening fold back ever so slightly. With great deliberation, he hooked his thumbs in the waistband of jeans and briefs, lowering them with infinite care, down his hips, pausing for more heartbeats than she wanted to count, before the big reveal.

Her breath caught in her throat. There's perfect and, *then there's perfect*. Tall like a sequoia, a champion body-builder's chest and arms would pale in comparison, narrow hips, muscled thighs and that erection… well, she didn't have words. He kicked his jeans off to the side and stood there, letting her look, just look.

Her mind whirled. She wasn't sure she could take much more of this. She needed his touch on her skin. Her heart pounded like distant thunder against the hills. She was so wet and ready for him. Two could play at this game. Kneeling on the bed she slipped one bra strap down, then the other, letting the garment drop to her waist. Slowly she unhooked it and tossed it to the corner. She saw his breath still and his erection salute her. She cupped her breasts in her hands, touching them with her thumbs so the nipples pebbled begging for his mouth to fondle them.

He took a step toward her. She held out her hand to stop him. He paused… waiting for what was to come next. Lauren stood, hooked her thumbs in her silken bikini pants, and eased them slowly down her hips and thighs before they too joined the pile of clothing in the corner. She knew the moment his control slipped and playtime was over. He walked to the bedside table and standing toe-to-toe, he opened a packet and rolled on protection.

They tumbled onto the bed, mouths devouring, hands gripping, skin against skin. He was inside her, filling her, their rhythms in sync with their pounding heartbeats. Her feminine walls pulsing around him. More, more, more. Faster, faster, faster. Release. Shattering. Replete. She knew this man. This was her man. The one meant for her.

Heart rates slowed, returning to a sustainable pace. She slipped slowly back to earth. He rolled them to their sides, legs entwined, pelvis to pelvis. She ran her hands lightly over his back while he nibbled at her neck. She moved in to kiss him and felt his smile against her lips.

"You are amazing. Beyond amazing. The Grand Canyon

of love-making." He huffed out a breath. "I don't take any of this lightly. To me making love is taking a step toward something real."

"Does that scare you?"

"Yeah, a little, but no regrets. I *want* to move forward with my life. With you. Feel whole again, not be a shadow of myself." He cupped her head in his hands and pulled her forward for a kiss. "But now, I think it's time for a shower. Want to join me?" His upturned lips and the light in his eyes held the promise of more than a shower.

Later, puttering in the kitchen, she smiled, thinking that's what a shower should be. Warm water cascading over two bodies that didn't need the extra heat. Fun. Laughter. Wondering what is it about sex and water that heightens every sensation. She didn't know, but maybe there was a research paper in there. If nothing else, she'd enjoy collecting the data.

He entered the kitchen and put his arms around her, pushing her hair aside to nuzzle her neck. Her heart zoomed across the horizon like a shooting star. His shell was cracking. She was sure of it.

"I thought maybe we should save the salmon you'd planned to grill for later when you get back from mending the fence. I found turkey slices in the fridge and made sandwiches. Hope that's alright?" She leaned back into him as she plated the food soaking up the closeness.

"I was going to ask if you could stay for dinner. Sounds like that's settled. Can you stay the night?" Kisses pattered like a spring shower down the column of her neck.

"Tempting, but I need to get home and take care of my dogs." She turned in his arms. "Next time I'll bring them with me."

"Next time. I like the sound of that." He rested his butt on one of the tall bar stools lining the raised counter. She sat beside him, their legs touching. "I won't be long with the fence. Do you want to come with me or stay here?"

"I think I'll stay here. I have notes to review on a client

I'm seeing on Monday. He lost his wife about a year ago and is having a hard time adjusting. I want to make sure I'm prepared. Work is one area of my life where I don't wing it."

"I'm not the only one having trouble getting over losing someone?"

"Far from it. The grief, the fear, the emptiness, the what-if questions, wondering if you ever can—or want to—love again." She shook her head. "Too often people let the emotions stay bottled up because it's difficult to talk to family and friends. They don't want to make anyone feel uncomfortable."

"My family has been great. Really supportive. I can talk to them about anything."

"But have you?"

He leaned back against the counter, but she could see the tension building in his shoulders.

"No, I guess not." "I'm not even sure *I know* what I'm feeling so how can I talk to anyone else about it?"

"That's where a trained counselor comes in. It's our job to help people dig down to the root causes." She rubbed her hand back and forth across his back. "Go mend that fence before you lose the daylight." She motioned with her head toward the door.

She walked him outside and retrieved her laptop from her car while he loaded supplies in his truck.

He pulled her to him. "I might need another shower when I get back."

"You let me know if you need someone to wash your back." The gentle teasing made her feel like she was walking on clouds.

"Be back in about an hour." He kissed her, climbed in his truck and drove off.

Back in the house the little library alcove off the entry called to her. She scanned his selection of titles and authors. Naturally, they were organized by genre and then alphabetized by author names. Historical, mystery/thrillers, sci-fi... unexpected, and poetry... really unexpected. She smiled when she saw the Harry Potter series. Nate had a whimsical side. Who knew? His collection suggested a penchant for stories where good battled evil and the hero stepped up and took charge.

She sat down in the leather wing chair and put her feet on the footrest. An unmarked, leather-bound book sat on the lamp table beside the chair. Out of curiosity, she picked it up. There in Nate's bold scrawl, lay his soul. Bare. On the page.

WANDERING

I go through the motions,
Knowing what I'm supposed to do and doing it,
But am I moving toward my dreams or away from them?
Dreams — elusive, vague, beyond my fingertips
I must know what I want if images swirl in my head
But do I?
Do I know?
If I did, wouldn't I grasp them in both hands
And pull myself forward
Instead of wandering, lost, alone?
Wouldn't I be working hard to make them happen?
I tell myself, I want to marry, have a family,
To live what my heart desires.
Then why does my gut clench in fear
When the possibility of love
Extends her hand to me?
Almost two years since my love joined the angels
Shouldn't I be ready to move on?
I'm rooted in place
I miss my love, but life goes on around me.
I'm not gaining ground, but not clinging to the past either,
If there is limbo, that's where I reside
Stuck in darkness with a piece of my soul missing.

She snapped the book shut. This was personal, private. She shouldn't read anymore. She set the book down in her lap. It fell open. A sign, right? She was meant to read what was on this page.

I TOUCHED HER HAND

I sat by her side, running my fingers down her arm.
The monitor had flat-lined seconds ago
Her parents stood silently weeping.
Her hand still warm in mine
But the life force I so desperately wanted to be there
Was no more.
Gone. Along with my heart, the joy of my life, my future,
Everything I'd ever wanted.
I don't know what to feel
Except that my life is out of my control.
Our life together was mapped out
College, career, marriage, home, children, old age.
It all seemed so simple, a logical progression
Then it wasn't.
I know I should be doing something
Comforting others, being strong, doing what needs to be done
That's my job. I'm the man. But I can't.
I can't think, I can't breathe, I can't feel,
I just can't.
Desolation.

A tear leaked from the corner of her eye and traced a track along her nose. She swiped it away and blew out a long breath. She snapped the book shut, set it on her lap, and again, it fell open. She moved to close it, saw the title, and couldn't resist.

LAUREN

Sunshine, joy, warmth, laughter, kindness,
Healer
My heart quickens when she walks into the room
The world… my world… is better for her
Her spirit of adventure lifts me up
To places I desperately want to go.

I reach out and touch her
And I feel the darkness giving way.
But fear, my ever faithful companion,
Turns my feet, dims the light.
Is there hope?
Can I accept what she offers?
What I crave more with each breath?
Help me Lauren,
Reach out your hand and pull me into the light.

She closed her eyes and tilted her head until it rested against the back of the chair. Slowly, with tenderness and care, she shut the book, smoothing the cover with a gentle touch. She sat, letting what she'd read seep into her heart, relishing the quiet. Footsteps. A quick intake of breath.

"What are you doing?" Nate's tone sharp as a paper cut. The kind where she immediately wanted to put the injured finger into her mouth and suck the pain away. An ominous quiet descended on the room.

Slowly she placed the book back where she found it. "I know I shouldn't have, but I didn't know what it was when I picked it up. I started reading and couldn't stop. Your words are beautiful, breath-taking. I closed it, I really did, but it opened again, like it wanted me to know what was inside. I didn't mean to read your poetry. I wasn't snooping. It just happened. The book was lying there beside your chair. I didn't read much. Only a few poems. Oh, Nate, I'm so sorry. I didn't mean to invade your private space..."

A number of emotions flickered across his face like one of those animated flip books. Annoyance, suspicion, uncertainty, anger, his fists clenched at his sides. "I need a minute." He stalked out the door.

She'd ruined everything. He had every right to be angry. She'd read his private journal, his inner-most thoughts without his permission. If she'd done this in her role as a therapist, it would have been unethical. As his lover, it was beyond unethical and ventured into the realm of betrayal.

Relationships had to be built on trust and honesty and respect or they were doomed to fail.

Peeking out the window, she saw him pacing, running his hand through his hair, silhouetted against a brilliant sunset, his body rigid. Panic lodged in her throat. What had she done? The barriers had finally started to crumble, and now this. The minutes ticked by, taut as a muscle with a cramp.

Finally the door opened. He leaned against the counter arms crossed over his chest, a muscle jumping along his jaw. "I'm pissed. No way around that. I trusted you. I told you things I haven't told anyone else. I let you in and this is how you repay me?" She couldn't have felt lower if he'd ground her into dust with his boot heel. His voice rumbled like distant thunder, announcing the pending storm.

"I've never shown my poems to anyone. Not even Sharon." His fists bunched at his sides. "I want to believe you. Believe you were caught in the moment and didn't mean to be cruel, but if I get to that point, it's going to take time."

"I am so sorry. Hurting you was not my intention." Guilt chased the words out of her mouth. "If it's any consolation, I only read a few, but they touched me." She placed one hand on top of the other across her heart. "They're beautiful, haunting. You have a gift." She went to him, resting her head against his chest, listening to the steady beat of his heart. When his arms came around her, she hoped they could work it out.

He set her away. "Like I said, I'm not ready yet. This is as close to a deal-breaker as it gets for me. I try to be honest and respectful of people. I expect the same in return." He turned his back to her. "I think it's best if you leave now. I've lost my appetite."

Lauren walked into the library and collected her purse and laptop, her heart thudding in her chest. She paused at the front door, glancing over her shoulder to see if he was watching. He wasn't. Her shoulders sagged and tears leaked down her cheek. Would it do any good to run to him, fall at his feet, and beg forgiveness? Not now. Nate needed space.

Time to think about the situation. Time to decide if he could find it in his heart to give her another chance. Quietly she closed the door behind her.

CHAPTER FOURTEEN

The elevator dinged and Lauren stepped into the hospital hallway, nerves bouncing in her belly like kids in a bounce house, wild and haphazard but without the joy. She followed the directions to the surgery waiting room. After the way they'd parted, she hadn't expected Nate to call her with the details of his father's surgery. He said it was to keep up the pretense. He didn't want his family to start asking questions. Still there was something in his voice, a vulnerability that gave her hope.

She paused a moment to calm her nerves and assess how Nate was doing. On the outside, he seemed like anyone else waiting to hear how a loved one did in surgery. A pinch of anxiety around his steel-blue eyes, huddled with others waiting news, speaking in hushed tones, sipping the ever-present bad hospital coffee—concerned but composed. On the inside, she suspected he was a mess. She could see it in the way he gripped his coffee creating tiny dents in the Styrofoam cup. An extra bit of tension bunching his broad shoulders. A restless shuffling of his feet. She could tell he was doing his best to hold it together. That's one of the things she admired most about him—his courage. He hated hospitals and the memories they held. Yet, he was here, supporting the people he loved.

Gloria June spotted her first and waved.

Nate looked up when his mom waved. Lauren's heart soared at his quick, warm smile, one that reached his eyes and relaxed his shoulders. Her heart plummeted a few seconds later when his face closed except for the hint of fear and wariness in his stance. Jeez, why didn't he just hold a string of garlic and cross in front of him. He wasn't ready to forget or forgive what she'd done. Frankly, she wasn't ready to forgive herself either.

She donned her cheerful mantle and approached the group. Showtime. Exchanging a hug and air kiss with Gloria June and a hug with Zach and Josh, she joined the circle. Grabbing Nate by his collar, she tugged him down to face level, and kissed him lightly on the lips. His eyes widened but his expression said he got the message. He needed to act like they were still together.

The grin that made her weak in the knees, returned. He hauled her into a tight embrace that lasted a little longer than was socially acceptable, but was more than fine with her.

When he released her, she kept a tight hold on his hand with one hand and clasped Gloria June's hand with the other. "How are you doing?"

"They took Jack into surgery about 15 minutes ago and expect him to be in recovery in about an hour. Now we wait," Gloria June said.

"Waiting's the hardest part. Not knowing what's happening, but Jack's strong and the procedure should make his life much better," Lauren said, squeezing Nate's hand.

"It'll be a few weeks before he can resume full activities," Gloria June said, "but we're expecting a full recovery and have him back good as new."

Gloria June linked her arm through Lauren's. "I need something other than this nasty coffee while we wait. What's say you and me check out the cafeteria?"

Lauren looked over at Nate and shrugged. He brought her hand to his lips and kissed it before releasing her. A quiver took up residence in midsection. She wished he meant the sweet gesture.

She and Gloria June stepped into the elevator and were quiet on the ride down. The squeak of rubber soled shoes on well-scrubbed linoleum, that faint, stale-air smell in the air, the general sense of people with a purpose followed them down the corridor. They didn't speak until they finished selecting food at the cafeteria and found a table.

"May I be frank with you?" Lauren asked.

"If you weren't, I'd be disappointed. What's on your mind?" Gloria June eyed Lauren over the top of her coffee mug.

"I'm concerned about Nate. I think his dad's surgery has upset him more than he's letting on." Lauren stabbed a piece of her omelet with her fork, but stopped short of her mouth, letting it hang in mid-air. "I'm a little worried—"

Gloria June's eyebrows rose in challenge.

Lauren grimaced. "A *lot worried* about Nate. He needs to talk to someone. Otherwise it will eat at him. What's been his reaction when you brought up seeing a counselor?" Lauren finally put the bite of food in her mouth.

Nate's mom set down her coffee and rolled her eyes. "What you'd expect. '*Mom, I'm fine, quit worrying.*' Sharing is not a personality trait that runs in the Kincaid male line."

"It's not just men. Most of us have trouble facing up to anything we perceive as weakness—especially ones we want to hide." She realized she'd continued to stir her coffee the entire time she spoke and set the spoon on the table with a tinny clatter. Nerves. It was important Nate got help. If he didn't deal with his issues, there was no chance for her to ever be more to him than a friend, and maybe not even that, since she'd betrayed his trust.

Gloria June pulled her attention back to the conversation. "As big and tough as he looks, he takes things hard. Jack's surgery has thrown him."

"Do you think it's shaken him enough to take the next step?" Lauren asked. Chairs scraped as the couple next to them got up.

Gloria June cocked her head and pursed her lips. "I hope so."

"Changing subjects, will you be okay managing the ranch for a while without too much help?"

"Ranching's in my blood, despite my parents' best efforts

to turn me into a lady."

"They were ranchers, and they didn't want you to be a rancher?"

"Like most parents, they wanted what they thought would be a better life for me so they tried to steer me a different direction. Sent me to private schools, made me be a debutant," she chuckled and the expression on her face suggested she was thinking of a distant memory. "When I need to, I can crook my pinkie finger with the best of them."

"To debutant sisterhood," Lauren said. The two exchanged one firm hand shake across the table.

"Anyway, when I married Jack, a rodeoer and a rancher, they sighed deeply, but accepted the inevitability because they knew I was happy."

"To finding the path in life that makes us happy." Lauren clinked mugs with Gloria June before pushing her empty plate away. "Should we pick up some food to take back to the guys?"

Gloria June glanced at her watch. "Yup, Jack should be out of surgery soon, and I want to be there when his doctor updates us."

****

Cold fingers of dread choked the air from his lungs. His early morning coffee churned like white water rapids in his stomach. He rubbed the back of his neck and paced. It surprised him that his mood changed the moment he spied Lauren entering the waiting area. She brought sunshine into his overcast world and calmed his jangled nerves—the ones that had been firing away like heavy rain on a tin roof. While the tension didn't completely disappear, it faded into the background of Lauren's smile.

"I thought you might be hungry." She handed him a plastic bag. Five minutes ago he would have sworn food was the last thing he wanted. The brush of her fingers as she gave him the bag, her fresh air scent mingling with the smell of eggs, bacon, and fried potatoes, turned the rapids in his stomach into a languid stream.

He took her hand, welcoming the electric sparks as flesh touched flesh, further distracting him from the near panic he'd felt a short time ago. They sat down on some chairs in the far corner of the room and he placed the food container on his lap. An involuntary groan escaped his lips when he opened the container and the full force of the breakfast smells hit him.

He tucked into the eggs over easy, polishing off the meal in record time. After he finished sopping up the last of the egg yolk with a piece of toast, he closed the lid and sat back with a contented sigh.

Lauren scooped up the container and bag and walked over to the trash. The easy sway of her hips reminded him of the hot, sweaty sex they'd shared a few days ago. She could make a man forget all his troubles, but the fear and sense of betrayal slithering around the edges mocked him.

The assessing gaze as she sat down and patted his knee, reminded him she was trained to read body language. From her expression, his must have hazard signs all over it. He tucked a loose strand of hair behind her ear, his fingers lightly grazing her cheek. So soft. If he could only sink into her caring arms and lose himself. He shook his head, and dropped his hand back to its resting place on his knee. Did he really still distrust her or was he using reading his poetry as an excuse to push her away?

"It shouldn't be long now." He saw the calculation in her eyes. "Tell me about calving and kidding season. What's it like for you?"

He knew she was distracting him but was happy to focus on other than his dad's surgery. "It starts with pre-birth vaccinations. After that, about three months answering calls to help with deliveries or disease. Sleep is a luxury. You have no idea how many cattle and goat operations exist in this area until the season hits from late March through early May."

"And horses, like the one I helped with, birth pretty

much any time?"

"Right, then there are the routine things we handle all year long—injury, disease. Even though we're mainly a large animal practice, we also see our share of small animals…" Nate jumped up as the doctor entered the waiting area. Together they hurried over to hear the news.

"Jack's doing fine. The operation went well. I'm not anticipating any issues. A nurse will let you know when the sedatives have worn off, which shouldn't be long, and then family can visit him in pairs. I expect to discharge him around noon tomorrow. Do you have any questions?"

"No, I think we're set." Gloria June clasped the doctor's hand. "Thank you so much for taking good care of my husband."

"You're welcome. He'll be back to his normal routine before you know it." The doctor turned and left.

Hugs and back slaps were shared all around, then Lauren pulled Nate to the side.

"I have clients this afternoon, so I'm going to take off now. I wish I could stay and keep you company, but I'm sure once you see your dad, you won't be as worried."

"I'm not worried." The words came out clipped. He stopped himself and drew in a calming breath. "Dad's tough. I know he'll be fine." He took her arm. "I'll walk you to your car." Nate called over his shoulder as they started toward the elevators, "I'll be right back."

She was quiet on the elevator ride down to the lobby and all the way to the parking structure. He could tell she had something on her mind. "You might as well spit it out."

"Spit what out?" He felt her tense beside him.

"Whatever it is you want to talk about, but aren't sure I do."

She sat on a nearby bench and patted the space beside her. "Are we going to talk about what happened at your ranch a little over a week ago, and whether or not we're going to keep up this charade?"

"It was nine days ago, to be exact." He bent forward

putting his head in his hands. She'd read his poetry without permission—and he had a right to be upset—but they'd also had mind-blowing sex. The first did not cancel out the second. No question, *his poetry was his to share.* She'd violated his trust, but which was more important? Stop seeing Lauren or clinging to his righteous anger? He suspected the problem wasn't anger, but the fact he was beginning to like her too much.

"Does it bother you that you didn't call me after we made love?"

Leave it to Lauren to get to the heart of the matter. "Yeah. Frustrates the hell out of me." He framed her face in his hands. "I'm still bothered by what you did, but I'd like to keep seeing you. Same agreement, nothing serious." He stuck out his hand. "Deal?"

She nodded. "Deal." Lauren gently rubbed his back. "Thank you for telling me about your dad's surgery."

"I wanted you here with me." He sat up and took her hand in his. It was true. He did want her here with him. She grounded him in ways he couldn't begin to understand.

She stood up and despite the warm spring weather he felt her shiver. The hurt in her eyes was a dagger to his heart. He realized if he ever wanted a serious relationship, one that fit like his favorite sweater, he needed help. When they got to her car, he wrapped her in his arms and kissed her. He knew what he had to do. As soon as he got home, he'd make an appointment with Jasmine. It was like he was buried in sand. He was tired of the suffocating feeling. It was time to rearrange his priorities.

CHAPTER FIFTEEN

Lauren needed to do something to take her mind off Nate. He hadn't contacted her since his dad's surgery a week ago. Volunteering for a good cause helped shift attention off her problems and on to helping someone else solve theirs. Besides what else was she going to do on a Saturday without a date? Work? She wasn't about to pull a Nate. She walked up to the receptionist's desk at the food bank warehouse and signed in.

The young Hispanic woman at the counter flipped the clipboard around and glanced down at the list of names. "Welcome, Lauren. We're so happy you could join us." She greeted Lauren with a warm smile and face full of dimples. "Our volunteers are just getting ready to carpool to the senior center. Follow me."

They rounded a corner and there stood Nate, chatting with the other volunteers. Everything inside her compressed like a coiled spring. She hadn't been expecting to see Nate. From the look on his face, he was just as surprised. The surprise was quickly replaced by a warm smile and softening in his blue eyes.

The Volunteer Coordinator looked from Lauren to Nate and back again. "You two know each other?"

"We're friends," Lauren replied with a lift of one shoulder.

"I have room in my truck. Why don't you ride with me?" Nate put his hand at Lauren's back and guided her to his truck. He opened the passenger side door for her and the extended cab door for the two older women, taking the time to help them clamber up.

Lauren twisted to face the two women in the back seat. "Hi, I'm Lauren." She shook hands with each woman as they introduced themselves.

"Gretchen," said the thin, grey-haired woman with a permanently pinched expression on her face.

"Darlene," said the roundish, woman with hair dyed the color of ripe rhubarb. "Haven't seen you before. Is this your first time?"

"First time at the senior center, but I've worked a few shifts stocking shelves in the warehouse."

"Well honey, we're glad you could join us," Darlene patted Lauren's hand. "And you're bound to be able to wield a knife better than the big lug beside you."

"Alright, ladies," Nate broke in. "Seat belts on?" He shifted the truck into gear and pulled out of the parking lot. "Besides, you know you only keep me around to do the grunt work."

"That, and you're darn cute to look at," Darlene purred.

Lauren's mouth dropped open in mock surprise. She glanced at Nate—whose ears were turning an endearing shade of pink—and stifled a chuckle behind her hand. He scowled at her but there was a twinkle in his eye. He took the good-natured ribbing in stride. This relaxed Nate was the one she hoped would stick around.

"You ladies behave back there or you're going to turn my head." Nate adjusted the volume on the radio. At the center, the first order of business was to unload the food and carry the bins into the kitchen. After that the chef lined them up around long, stainless steel counters and got them busy peeling and chopping. Some were moved to the ranges and stirred the ingredients in industrial-sized pots.

Nate was the designated heavy lifter. He hefted the bins of ingredients and placed them on the working counters. He pulled stacks of plastic cafeteria trays out of cupboards and set them out on the dining room side of the long, glassed-in counter where the food would be ladled on to the seniors' plates. He carried the large pots from the stove and transferred the contents into the metal tubs in the buffet.

Trying not to be too obvious, Lauren observed him out of the corner of her eye. The play of muscles in his broad back, his easy grace, the way his jeans sat low on his hips and outlined his muscled thighs was a bonus she hadn't expected when she'd signed up to volunteer. Her heart melted at the laugh lines framing his eyes, the friendly pats and touches he shared with his fellow volunteers, and the way he jumped in to help if someone was struggling.

When the seniors filed in, Nate was at the head of the service line greeting regulars by name, asking how they were doing, commenting on anything new and different about them. He had a great way with people. One more thing she admired about him.

Dinner service over, the volunteers grabbed mops and cleaning rags and scoured until the kitchen returned to his pre-meal shine. Chores complete, everyone carpooled back to the food bank.

Nate lingered after Gretchen and Darlene wandered off. Fire shot up her arm when he captured her hand in his. Their lips touched briefly.

"Want to get a cup of coffee?" he asked. "We should be seen together if we want people to continue thinking we're together."

For a second, hope bloomed. Then he added the last part and she chilled faster than a blast of air conditioning down her neck. "I know you've been busy," Lauren said. "Are you sure you have time?" She could tell by the way the muscles bunched along his jaw, he'd heard the frustration in her voice. Sighing, she pushed the disappointment aside and focused on him. She was not a whiny, clingy person and their dating obviously meant nothing to him. "Coffee would be great. How's your dad?"

"Getting more restless every day. He sees the doctor tomorrow, and we're all hoping he gets the green light to get back to his normal routine. If not, my mother might strangle him." He framed her face in his hands and looked into her eyes. "I know you're upset we haven't gone out lately. I've been working stuff out. I want to see you again. Clear the air. What are you doing next week?"

"I leave for Los Angeles on Friday and have to squeeze all my clients appointments into the next six days—meaning I'm even working tomorrow. How about the weekend after that?" Talk about rotten timing. If he wanted to talk, she hated postponing it, but it couldn't be helped. Her body felt like she'd walked outside into 90% humidity.

"I'd forgotten you were going out of town. I'll email you while you're gone and we'll figure something out."

She wanted to ask what he meant by 'working stuff out', but Nate's phone rang.

He pulled it out of his pocket, looked at the display, and his mouth thinned. "Work." He swiped the screen to answer. "Coffee will have to wait." He turned his back and made arrangements to meet a client at the clinic.

"Another emergency?" She knew his work had to come first. It's part of who he was and he had debts hanging over his head. Dang it though, a small, selfish part of her wanted to be just as important to him as his work.

"Yeah. Sue Ann is at her daughter's pre-school play and I offered to fill in for her if a call came in after my volunteer shift."

The disappointment she saw in his face eased the heavy lump in her chest. "Maybe it's time we called off our arrangement." He started to speak and she reached up and touched his lips. "It could just be temporary. You have every right not to trust me, but until you decide whether or not you want to keep seeing me, I don't want to be tied down."

"I still want to see you when you get back from Los Angeles. You willing?"

She nodded. It was up to him. He had to forgive her if they had any hope of moving on.

****

Nate wiped his sweaty palms on his jeans. He'd finally made an appointment with Jasmine. Was it too late to make a mad dash for the door? No, if he didn't do something, he was going to lose Lauren. He didn't expect much out of this visit, but he wanted to change and was willing to give it a try. If this didn't work, he had no idea what would.

He stood and walked the clipboard with the new patient information over to the receptionist. New patient. Is that what he was? Did that imply he was sick? That there was something wrong with him? No, that would indicate weakness and he wasn't weak. He was fine. He only needed a little help figuring out how to deal with some stuff.

The receptionist smiled up at him as he handed her the paperwork. He returned the smile though it fell short of his usual high octane wattage. He looked around at the cozy waiting room with its sets of homey sofas and chairs carefully arranged to allow patients to have some privacy. Soft lighting, green plants, neutral paint on the walls. He figured it was meant to help him relax. Fat chance of that. Nerves pinged through him like moths against a light bulb.

"Hi Nate." A gentle touch patted his shoulder. He felt himself flinch, but with effort kept his startle reflex to a minimum. "Sorry to have kept you waiting. Come on into my office," Jasmine said.

Nate turned, facing the statuesque black woman, a thin-line smile on his lips, his heart pounding like he'd just settled onto the back of a bucking bronco and the chute was about to open. "Hi Jasmine, or do I call you Dr. Masters. Not sure of the protocol."

"Jasmine is fine. Would you like some water?"

"I'm good." He realized he'd been jiggling the coins in his pockets as they walked. With as much nonchalance as he could muster, Nate let his hands dangle at his sides.

She motioned to a pale green overstuffed chair. He sat and propped a booted foot on his knee, one hand gripping his ankle to keep his foot still. Jasmine sat opposite him across a low, square table. She crossed her legs at the knee and placed the paperwork in her lap.

"I understand you've lived in the San Antonio area all your life."

"Except for college and a year in the Peace Corps. Kincaids have lived here for more than 100 years."

"That's a lot of history. Tell me what keeps you here."

"Family. Work. I like it here." Maybe this wasn't going to be as hard as he thought, but didn't see how talking about where he lived was going to make a difference.

"Tell me about your family."

"I've got a mom, dad, two brothers, a gazillion aunts, uncles, cousins." He shrugged. Why did she need to know this stuff?

"That's a lot of people. Do you get along with your family?"

"Most of the time." Where was she going with this? She was supposed to help him get over his anxiety. Wave that magic wand or whatever it was therapists did to make the problem go away.

"Tell me about a time you didn't get along with your family."

Blank like a page in his journal before he started a poem. Emotions. Impressions. Flashes of insight. "A lot of people with opinions about how to live my life." He wasn't sure where that came from, but he might as well run with it. Do what Lauren said and go with his gut.

"How do folks think you should live your life?" Her pen poised over her legal pad, waiting.

His mind scrambled wondering how to put it into words. Words that expressed feelings. What *did* he feel? He knew she was waiting, but oddly something about her didn't pile on the pressure to respond quickly. Calm. Reassuring. Like Lauren.

"Sometimes it's better if you don't analyze your response too much." Her voice low and soothing. "Just say what comes to mind."

He took a deep breath, let the foot resting on his knee

drop to the floor as he leaned forward, a hand on each knee. He could recite these in his sleep. "In no particular order… I should have joined the NFL instead of becoming a vet. I should have married Sharon as soon as I graduated instead of taking off for the Peace Corps. I should have joined an existing practice instead of going into debt to build my own. I sure don't need that big house if I don't have a wife and a passel of kids to fill it. And, it's time I stopped dawdling and find myself a good woman. Sharon's been dead almost two years. It's time to move on." One heel tapped a soft staccato rhythm on the carpet.

"Are they right? Do you regret any of the decisions you've made?"

"With what I knew then, I'm pretty sure I'd make the same choices today. Maybe if I'd known time would run out before I could marry Sharon." He scrubbed his hands over his face. "I don't know."

"Tell me a little about Sharon."

"She was diagnosed with brain cancer shortly after we were engaged and died within six months—two months before our wedding date. Watching her suffer… it was the worst time of my life. I don't think I could do that again." The hollowness became a sharp ache encased by dread poking him with tiny sticks.

"That's what happened. Tell me about her. Who was she as a person?"

Was. So final. Gone. Past. Done. "My rock. Clear-eyed and practical." A smile tilted his lips and a stillness like moonlight washed through him. "Sweet. Something about her always made me think of the first flowers of spring. Unexpected beauty." A lump the size of a grapefruit lodged in his throat. He shook his head. No more words.

Jasmine leaned forward. Her touch on his arm supportive. "Cherish those memories." When she sat up, she shuffled the file folder so it was on top of the legal pad and opened it. "You said the issue you want to address is the anxiety you have about getting involved in a serious relationship. Is that a correct assessment?"

"Yeah, that's it." He paused and swept a hand through his hair. "I want to have a family someday…" He rubbed the back of his neck. How do women do it? Share their feelings all the time. "Thought I'd see what you could do."

"I think I need to clarify how therapy works." She folded her hands in her lap. "I'm not the one who is going to make you less anxious. You are. I'll help you explore why you're reacting the way you are and provide techniques to help you minimize the impact of anxiety and grief, but you'll be the one looking inside yourself and discovering what's holding you back."

Nate took a deep breath. Fear encased his lungs like a shell around a Brazil nut. Tough to crack. What if he was an emotional wasteland? What if there was nothing to figure out? Maybe he'd had his one shot at love and that was all he had in him.

She handed him a standard, black composition notebook. "I want you to keep this journal and write down the following…"

Nate retrieved a pen from his pocket and started to open the notebook.

"You don't need to write this down. Everything I am going to tell you is already printed out and in the journal. I'm simply going over the information in case you have any questions.

Nate nodded. Couldn't believe he was going to do this touchy-feely stuff. Told him something about how important Lauren was becoming to him.

"I want you to make note of the following—when anxiety takes over, write down what you were doing and what thoughts were going through your mind. I also want you to tell me what you do right after you feel anxious to make the feeling go away. Finally, I want you to pull out photos of Sharon and write down what you remember. How they make you feel. Any questions so far?"

"What if I can't think of anything?" He looked down at

the notebook as he flipped the blank pages and felt anxiety mount. He hadn't looked at photos of Sharon since the funeral. Could he face the memories? The only place he let his feeling out was through his poetry—and he wasn't about to share that. What if what he wrote made him sound like an idiot?

As if reading his thoughts, Jasmine said, "This isn't a writing competition. It's an opportunity to learn more about yourself. Think of it as a journey. Don't expect the wall you've built to come down overnight."

"Okay." He could hear the uncertainty and skepticism in his voice, but Jasmine seemed to take it in stride.

"Next task. When you start feeling anxious, I want you to breathe slowly and try to relax until the anxiety subsides. Let's practice the breathing and relaxation for a minute so you understand how it should feel."

They practiced the exercise for a few minutes and then Jasmine continued, "Finally, meditation is helpful. You might even consider doing yoga with Lauren."

He narrowed his eyes. "Isn't yoga for girls?"

"Not at all. Lots of men practice yoga, and trust me, after your first time on the mat, your body will tell you yoga is not for sissies."

"Won't I look silly?" When Lauren had suggested he do yoga with her, he'd gone online and looked at pictures of men doing yoga. Some of the poses didn't look very manly and others he figured he'd fall flat on his face and embarrass himself. That's not the way a real man behaved.

"Everyone feels a little self-conscious at first." She put her pad and pen on the table. "Lauren teaches couples yoga. I think having a private session with her would ease your concerns. I'm sure she would be happy to work with you."

"But won't she wonder why I'm interested?"

Has she ever asked you to do yoga with her?"

"Yeah."

"Have you seen her in her yoga outfit?"

"Yeah." He felt like he was walking into a trap and it was

about to snap shut on his leg.

"And did you like the way she looked?"

"I see where you're going." He sighed. "She looked sexy as hell."

"There you have it. You could always say you saw an article on men's health saying it was a great stress reliever and you'd like to give it a try."

"I'll think about it."

"For now, the breathing and relaxation exercises will help. Let's schedule your next week's appointment." She got up and walked over to her computer while Nate pulled out his phone. Once they'd set the date and time, she walked him out.

On the way to his truck, Nate decided he would check out this yoga stuff. Maybe he was letting preconceptions about what it was get in his way. Like so much else in his life? Was he bothered by what people might think? Or was he afraid of getting close to Lauren? It was time to step outside his comfort zone. He pulled out his phone and sent an email to Lauren.

CHAPTER SIXTEEN

Lauren entered the hand-blown glass shop and felt her spirits lift like a balloon bouncing along on a playful air current. Because she was leaving at the end of the week for her Los Angeles trip, her schedule had been jam packed. A long lunch with Ashley made for a nice break. Ashley probably needed the break as much as Lauren did. Not only had her parents visited recently, but she'd worked up the courage to introduce Zach to them. Things must be getting serious between them.

She spotted Ashley examining a fabulous oval platter in exquisite shades of blue, tilting it this way and that to let the light frolic across its surface. Lauren paused by one of the pedestal displays to admire a marbled yellow and orange vase with whimsical red, daisy-like, glass flowers peeking over its rim.

Ashley gently placed the platter back on the glass table, caressing its satiny finish with her fingers. "What do you think?" she asked as Lauren came to stand beside her.

"It's breathtaking. Reminds me of Van Gogh's sky painting." Lauren traced one of the swirls with her finger. "It would look great on your breakfast table."

"You're right." She turned to the clerk. "I'll take it. Can you hold it for me until after lunch?"

"Sure can." The clerk took Ashley's credit card and picked up the platter. "I'll wrap it for you and hold it at the counter. I'll be right back with your receipt."

"After the disaster of my parents' visit, I deserve a treat." Ashley signed the slip of paper the clerk handed her.

"Is your mother speaking to you yet?" Lauren rubbed a circle on Ashley's back.

"Not yet. She needs to properly chastise me first." Ashley looked heavenward and shook her head.

"Ready for lunch?" Lauren asked. A walk in the sunshine would make them both feel better. They pushed through the glass doors and stepped out onto the pebbled walkways of the Riverwalk to stroll along the tree-lined path beside the channeled river.

A few blocks later they reached one of the arched stone footbridges spanning the river. Lauren stopped and rested her forearms on top of the bridge railing. She gazed down at the slow-moving water and the colorful water taxis shuttling people up and down the river. Across the bridge, tables with brightly-colored umbrellas invited diners to stop and relax. Bright flowers and lush greenery filled an abundance of planters.

"Do you think the way mother treats me will ever stop being hurtful?" Ashley asked. Her sigh sounded like she was finally beginning to release the disappointment Lauren knew was pricking at her like a cactus thorn.

"Not a chance. You're kind and generous. You have a heart. The guilt she lays on you is designed to make you feel like less than you are." Lauren bumped her friend's shoulder with her own. "I'm proud of the way you're moving on and taking charge of your life."

They continued on to the restaurant and took a vacant table for two along the water's edge. The server brought them a basket of bread, handed them the menus, and promised someone would be with them shortly.

"I'm glad to hear Zach took your parents in stride. She can make people want to slink away with their tail between their legs."

"I'm proud of him. He took everything she threw at him and landed on his feet. I'm reassessing my first impressions. He may be forever material after all." Ashley idly tossed a chunk of bread to the ducks bobbing in the water near their table. "Are you and Nate making any progress?"

"Baby steps." Lauren absently smoothed the area around her plate with her hands before continuing. "Lately he's made a point of staying in touch and we've actually had a date at least once a week. Sometimes it feels forced, like I'm an assignment he needs to check off a list, instead of something he *wants* to do."

"Think he's seeing Jasmine?"

"That's my guess, but I'm not going to ask. He'll tell me if he wants to." Lauren paused listening to the gentle lapping of the river against the concrete canal walls and the soft quacking of the ducks. She'd made such a mess of things and was thrilled Nate was giving her another chance. "I don't want to be an assignment, something he has to do. I want to be the person he can't wait to be with." The same way she couldn't wait to be with him. She'd always thought she was a self-contained person, but when she was with Nate, she felt like she did after a big Thanksgiving dinner—full, happy, and loved. Her life had been missing something important.

Ashley leaned forward and grabbed Lauren's hand. "That sounds serious. Where did my '*I'm never going to be tied down*' friend go?"

Lauren cringed. She hadn't meant to say that, but she knew it came from an authentic place. She'd fallen for Nate. "I want to be the love of his life. This pretend relationship is wearing thin."

Ashley released Lauren's hand and sat back. "Do you really think it's all still pretend on his part? I mean, it's been months since he suggested this and you're still seeing each other."

"Four, but who's counting?" Lauren said. She rested her elbows on the table and propped her chin in her hands. "You could be right. He may be coming around." The butterflies in her stomach took flight.

Ashley rubbed her palms together in excitement. "Spill, girlfriend."

"Nate asked about doing yoga with me. Said he'd read

about couples yoga in some men's magazine and thought it sounded interesting. Wondered if I could teach him a few moves."

"Get out of town," Ashley shrieked loudly enough for a few heads to turn their direction. She put her hand over her mouth and lowered her voice. "I'll *bet* you could teach him a few moves. So are you going to?" She smiled and wiggled her eyebrows.

"When I get back from Los Angeles."

Ashely glanced at her watch. "I've got to be going. When do you leave?"

"On Friday. I'll be back the following Friday. I've tacked on a few extra days to visit my brother and sister while I'm there."

"How are Daphne and Ben?"

"Loving LA and loving their work. Ben's been assigned to draw one of the lead characters in a feature animated film so his head's in the clouds right now. Daphne is the assistant to the lead designer on a new textile line and can't talk about anything else."

I'm glad they're doing well."

The two hugged. "When I get back, Nate and I have a yoga date. Make or break time." The man was either going to bend or they would end their arrangement—and she would be free to date other people.

****

Nate slapped the paper-covered notebook against his knee, waiting for Jasmine to get settled. He was eager to begin their session. He felt like he'd made a lot of progress over the past five weeks. Lauren was due back from Los Angeles and he planned to tell her he'd been seeing Jasmine.

Jasmine looked up from reviewing his file and smiled. "From the smile on your face, I suspect you've got news to share."

He took a sip of the fruit-infused water he'd brought.

Another one of the things he'd done in his quest to open himself to new experiences.

"I think I've made a break through. The past weeks have been some of the most difficult in my life—looking back at the past and digging into what I felt after my grandparents' deaths," he drew in a deep breath, "and more importantly, Sharon's."

"Tell me what you learned."

His heart pounded and he felt like he'd eaten something that didn't quite agree with him. He'd always thought of himself as strong and brave. The last few weeks as he'd slowly gone through photos of Sharon, he'd looked in the mirror and seen the coward he was. "I'd been running from my life. Once Sharon died, I locked away anything that reminded me of her. Until I compared how I reacted to my grandparents' deaths with Sharon's, I hadn't realized I'd never dealt with either loss." His fingers dug into the arm of the padded chair.

"The term you're looking for is closure. What is it about your grandparents' deaths that made it difficult for you to deal with Sharon's death?" The paper rustled as she quietly folded the top page behind the others.

His throat tightened. It wasn't easy talking about emotions he'd buried deep inside. "It upset me to watch my grandmothers suffer after their husbands died. While this may not be a medical term, I'd swear they died of broken hearts. Is that possible?"

"Yes, broken heart syndrome is real. Studies of couples over 50, show that surviving spouses have a 66% higher risk of dying within three months of their partner."

"So it's not an old wives tale?"

"Not at all. Our reaction to grief can produce both psychological and physical responses."

"After my grandmothers' deaths, I began to believe, *if you truly love your spouse, you will want to die when they do*." His voice whooshed out on a whisper. "When Sharon died, *I didn't want to die*." Guilt pinched his lungs. "Maybe I hadn't loved her enough. Maybe I *couldn't* love enough." He swiped a hand across his eyes, embarrassed by the moisture gathering there. "I'm a man. Emotions aren't supposed to control me, but I felt like I was caught in an avalanche, tumbled around, out of control."

"I think you know that none of that is true. Let me ask you something. Do you regret having your grandmothers or Sharon in your life?" Jasmine's calm gaze encouraged him to continue.

"No, not at all." He sat up straighter, ready to battle falsehood.

"Do you remember what you wrote in your list of things you're grateful for? What did you gain by loving them?"

He crossed his arms over his chest and looked up at the ceiling taking his time to answer. "Joy. Happiness. The warmth of unconditional love. Strength. A desire to be a good person, to make the world better because they made me better."

"That's a lot of powerful emotions. Was loving them worth the loss and pain you experienced?"

"Yes, and that leads me to my breakthrough. Writing down my negative feedback loops and why they weren't true, made me face some things."

"What did you learn?" Her pen scratched quietly over the paper.

"When I tell myself 'love always ends in loss,' I had to acknowledge that most of the people I love are still alive. Those who did die? If they hadn't been in my life, I wouldn't be the person I am now. I've reached the point where I want to choose happiness." Nate sat back and put his splayed hands on his thighs. It was hard to believe how free he felt, like the stone inside his chest had crumbled to dust.

"What about your other negative feedback loop?" Her eyebrows arched in question.

"That I will never fall in love again?" He wasn't sure he should say what had popped into his mind. He shrugged, why not? Jasmine was a good sounding board. "I think I'm falling in love with Lauren. Beginning to believe I can build a life with her." Until he met Lauren, he'd known something was missing, but he ignored it, assuring himself he was fine. He'd avoided feeling too deeply. Now he understood how barren his life had been. The only problem was how did he move past their bogus relationship and create a real one?

"Moving forward, what changes do you see yourself making?"

"There will always be a place in my heart for Sharon, but I want a real live, breathing woman in my arms, not a ghost. Loving another woman won't diminish what I had with Sharon." He sandwiched his hands between his knees and looked down at his feet. "I've been telling Lauren about Sharon and you're right, it's opened up places I'd been afraid to examine." He'd been trying to protect everyone around him and denied the pain. If he didn't share it, it must not be real.

"That's what we've been working toward, but I'll caution you, your old behavior patterns have been with you a long time. Don't be surprised if you occasionally slip backwards. Know that your fears may never completely disappear, but also know *you* have the power to control how you respond."

"I understand I've still got work to do, but for the first time in a long time, I think maybe I can get past this."

CHAPTER SEVENTEEN

The tingle along the base of her skull told Lauren she was being watched as she pulled into Nate's driveway for their yoga date. She'd returned to San Antonio yesterday afternoon and was delighted she hadn't had to wait long to see him. The front door jerked open before she'd put the car in park. Nate bounded down the steps, his dogs trotting at his heels. The two Australian Cattle dogs streaked forward to greet her.

"I'm glad you brought your dogs." He nodded to the pair in her backseat, noses pressed against the window. "That means you won't have to rush off later."

"I thought it was time our pets got acquainted. She opened the door and let her two Golden Retrievers out. The dogs immediately started sniffing noses and other parts. Moving to the back of her car, she lifted the hatch.

He struck a pose, arms outstretched to his side as he turned around, shaking his manly rear end. "Will this do for my first yoga session?"

Oh, yeah her brain sang. Getting her body to relax into the poses might prove challenging today. Nate in a pair of cutoff sweats and a tank top, took her breath away. The sweats pulled taut against his muscled thighs and bunched over his family jewels in a most intriguing way. Exactly what he could do with those jewels had lightning bolts zinging through her body. The shirt caressed his muscled chest. Bulging, tree-trunk arms lay bare to appreciative eyes. Back muscles rippled as he turned, lifted his arms, and flexed his biceps.

She swallowed the lust in her throat. "Very nice. You look ready to do some good stretching."

"Stretching? *How much stretching*?" He followed her to the back of the car. "I'm not going to have to do the splits, am I?" He peeked inside the back of her Honda CRV like monsters lurked within.

Lauren slapped the rolled yoga mats against his chest. His arms automatically closed around them. She lightly patted his cheek. "I promise we won't do anything that hurts—much." She handed him a beach bag and grabbed a small boombox, then strolled toward the house.

She knew exactly what part of her anatomy he was admiring and emphasized the hip action. Pausing inside the entry, she turned to him, "where would you like to have your first session?"

His free hand swept down her side caressing the bare skin below her sports bra top and stopped at her waist. "Don't suppose you'd consider my bedroom an appropriate place to work out?"

His expression was wicked hot and very tempting. She wasn't going to rule that option out, but yoga first to work on those trust issues.

"I doubt the workout you have in mind would be relaxing." She lowered her eyes so he wouldn't see the longing there. Him, her in that big bed of his upstairs. She gave herself a mental head slap.

"The end result would be relaxing—but hot and sweaty would come first." He raised his brows as though proud of his comeback.

She crossed her arms and gave him 'the eagle eye.' The one that made her big, he-man brothers turn tail and run.

"Killjoy. How about in the backyard? Nice view of the swimming pool and pond. Out in nature, all that stuff." He shrugged, his hands in front of him palms up. "The grass would make for a soft landing, if needed."

"Good choice." She framed his face with her hands, his stubble raspy against her palm. "Don't worry, I'll catch you if you fall. Couples yoga is about trust." He led the way outside.

Lauren gazed around the yard and off to the horizon. Her breathing regulated. She visualized her muscles lengthening and flowing into the poses. She sensed Nate behind her. The mats hit the ground with a soft thud. His hands came to rest on her shoulders and she leaned into his solid frame.

"Did you hydrate, no caffeine, like I asked?"

"Yes, ma'am. The things I'll do for you." His deep voice vibrated against her back, mirroring her hushed timbre.

She hoped this was the first step in things he was willing to do for her. Speculation at the possibilities in their future curled around her heart, irresistible in their allure.

"Let's get started. Please roll out the mats so they touch. In the shade of that tree would be nice." She walked over to the beach bag, pulled out two towels. Peaceful water sounds flowed from the boombox.

"In yoga we listen to our bodies. Nothing you do should cause pain. The stretching should be natural, a release of muscles and tension. We'll start by sitting cross-legged on the mat facing each other."

Nate sat down in the middle of the mat.

"We need to touch, so scoot closer." Once he was in position, she said, "Close your eyes and feel your mind and body relax."

She took his left hand and placed it over her heart, then put her left hand over his. Their right hands joined in a Namaste prayer pose in front of them. "Breathe slowly. Feel our heartbeats become one." The oneness surrounded her. The merging of psyches. She wanted to pour hope and healing from her into him and diminish his emotional pain.

"Open your eyes." Slowly, she leaned forward, kissing him tenderly on the lips. She saw peace and calmness nestle in his eyes—and wonder as well.

"Shift around so we're back-to-back. Press your spine against mine. Place your hands in front of you on the floor and walk your hands forward as far as is comfortable and I'll arch against you." The powerful muscles across his shoulders and down his spine lengthened against her back rippling like tall grass in a breeze. Sensual. Sultry. "Breathe in and exhale through the stretch." Molding herself to him gave her a wonderful stretch across her chest and midriff.

"We are going to reverse the process." Leaning forward, she welcomed his weight, happily supporting him. "Sit up again and tuck yourself into a ball. Rest your forehead on the floor and relax your arms beside your body." She kneeled beside him carefully guiding his movements. "Comfortable?"

"Mmm," he murmured.

"This is called the child's pose. I'm going to climb on your back and do the same pose on top of you." She surrendered to the joy and closeness of the moment, her cheek resting between his shoulder blades. Lauren slid her hands down his arms and rested them on the floor beside his head. A contentment poured through her as she sheltered him with her peace. She eased first one leg and then the other over the curve of his buttocks and stood. She waited while he unfurled his tall frame from the floor.

"Now we switch places."

"Are you kidding? I'll *crush* you." His eyebrows shot up in surprise.

"No you won't. Let go and trust me." Her hands slipped up and down his bare arms, tracing the contours of his deltoids and biceps.

He nodded and once she folded into the child pose, climbed on her back. He was heavy, a good heavy. It was calming being blanketed by him. She felt the loss of his warm presence as soon as he moved away. She kissed him softly. "Thank you for your trust."

He stepped back, hands on hips, inhaling slowly, exhaling slowly. "When you said yoga would build trust and connection, I thought you were exaggerating."

Lauren joined their hands, in front of their chests and gazed deeply into his steel-blue eyes.

"We'll stretch our sides next. You stand here." She placed her hands on his hips and moved him, then stood beside him a few feet away. "Reach over your head with your right hand and grasp my left arm." She extended her arm over her head angling it toward him. "Put your left hand on my hip and push outward. We'll pull toward each other with our other arm creating an inward arc with our bodies."

The top of their heads touching, breathing in unison, the easy pressure of his hand on her hip, arms twining overhead... a sensation like no other. He was part of her now. Wistfulness, like a soft spring rain, trickled down her body bathing her in tenderness. Did he feel the same? Was she a part of him?

They released and stretched the other side.

"For our final pose, you need to lie on your back, knees to your chest. I'll do a backbend over you r feet and then you'll lift me in the air."

"Are you sure about this? What if I drop you?"

"Worst case, I tumble onto the grass from a few feet in the air. That's not going to happen though. I trust you."

He lay on his back. She pressed her butt into his feet and arched back. Slowly he raised her. She felt a glorious stretch through her abdominals and the luxury of floating free, all because of this man. She closed her eyes and felt the breeze against her skin. Placing her hands on either side of his head. she kicked out of the backbend into a handstand before lowering to her feet.

Nate stood up. Their lips met. The kiss lingered, creating a buoyant glow in her chest. They were in another world. Lauren picked up one of the towels, smoothing it tenderly over his face, around his neck and down each arm. He returned the favor with another towel. He bent and scooped up the mats and rolled them in tight cylinders. She retrieved the boombox and beach bag. He draped an arm across her shoulders and pulled her close to kiss her neck. Together they walked back into the house.

CHAPTER EIGHTEEN

Nate tossed the mats on the kitchen island and relieved Lauren of the boombox and beach bag. Who knew yoga could be such a turn on? Sure had him ready to forget the rest of the world existed and spend the day making slow, passionate love to her. He moved to take her in his arms. She held up her index finger in a wait-a-minute gesture. Damn, maybe he'd read this whole thing wrong. He would have bet she was as ready for some time between the sheets as he was.

"There's one more thing we need to do before your session is complete."

"I'm perfectly happy with the way things ended. Can't we skip whatever this last bit is?" He reached for her again. She gracefully dodged him.

"Nope. You need the whole experience." She pulled a couple towels, a small bottle of something, and a few candles out of her bag. "Your bedroom will do nicely for this last experience." She walked a few steps and glanced back over her shoulder. "You coming?"

He felt like a puppy scampering after her, tripping all over his feet in his haste to catch up. The swing of her hips as she moved up the stairs called to him like a siren song.

"Take off your clothes." He liked the sound of that. "And lie face down on the bed."

She set the candles around the room and closed the shutters as he undressed and lay face down on the bed. He heard the flick of a lighter. A faint citrus scent crept into the room. The bed dipped as she straddled him. The scrape of a bottle on his nightstand, hands rubbing rapidly together and then—

heaven.

Soft hands slick with oil, kneaded his shoulders, her thumbs sweeping up his neck. Next the heel of her hand lightly glided up his spine from waist to neck. He felt a trickle of oil on his back. She placed her hands over the oil to warm it, then splayed hands rubbed circles outward from his spine to his ribs—pressing and kneading. Her touch drifted over his skin light as a hummingbird, numbing his mind to everything except her. She scooted lower, massaging his glutes, pressing with her thumbs, down his legs in long strokes. When she reached his feet, his body floated on a warm tropical sea. He wanted to position her beneath him and take her, but his limbs were beyond obeying his brain's command.

"Turn over." Her voice seemed to come from a million miles away yet from a place near his epicenter. She knelt above his head and leaning forward worked on his pectorals, sweeps of hand from sternum to ribs and down to his abdominals. She moved off the bed and he missed being cradled by her thighs. Her magic touch focused on his legs and his feet once more, thumbs pressing into spots that made him want to growl with contentment or whimper with surrender.

She moved away. He heard the rustle of clothing and opened his eyes in time to see her pull the sports bra over her head and shimmy out of her yoga pants. Naked. His male parts shifted into high alert, but the rest of him was too lethargic to do more than enjoy the show.

Her next move surprised him, in a thrilling, please-don't-stop way. She nudged his legs apart and knelt between them. Her breasts dangled like low-hanging fruit in front of him begging for his touch. He obliged, cupping their fullness in his hands, running his thumbs along their underside and through the valley they created. Her hands swept up his inner thigh and over the crease that joined legs to torso, but didn't touch the part of him panting for the stroke of her hands. Sweet torture. When she finished with his legs, she cupped his balls, gently massaging them. The pleasure center of his brain erupted.

Reaching up, he tangled his fingers in her silky hair, pulling her down onto his chest. Their lips met, the kiss languorous, confident, drugging in its restrained passion. The oil that remained on him heightened the sensation of skin gliding caressingly over skin, like air whispering over heated bodies. He couldn't get enough of touching her and he planned to devote attention to every inch of her body.

Thumbs traced slow circles on her temple as he held her head in place and they sank into another kiss. Tongues tangled with each other. Exploring, tasting, remembering. He drew the fresh air scent of her deep into his lungs. He traced the outline of her lips with the tip of his tongue. Gentle kisses started at the corner of her mouth, across her cheek and ended at the hollow beneath her ear. He nibbled and nuzzled his way from her earlobe to the base of her throat.

Rolling to put himself on top and bracing on his arms, he bent for another lingering kiss. His hands cupped her breasts, his thumbs teasing her nipples into tight buds. Kisses trailed down her throat to the top of her breasts before he suckled the waiting nibs. He felt her writhing beneath him, squirming with pent up desire. Anticipation rocketed through him, but he planned to do so much more to her before they both achieved release.

His lips worked their way down her midriff, to her abdomen, before circling her navel with his tongue. His hands slid up the smooth skin of her inner thigh, caressing and kneading as he kissed the tender skin beside her most feminine part. She was hot and ready, the scent of desire in the air.

When he entered, he eased in slowly, determined to draw out their lovemaking. He buried himself to his hilt in her moist, hot core. Stilled. Savoring the sensation of being surrounded by her soft heat. Her delicious sighs almost threw him over the edge. His arms shook with the effort to hold back. Together they fell into an undulating rhythm, the pace gradually swelling like the crest of a wave until her cushiony walls clenched around him and they sped to the other side... in tandem.

They stayed locked together until he rolled to his side so they faced each other. He traced the curve of her hip with his palm as he leaned forward for another kiss.

"You've destroyed me. I don't think I'll be able to move for days. Just have to stay right here." He massaged her scalp with his fingertips.

"Hmmm, me either." Lauren rolled onto her back and snuggled closer.

Stroking her hair away from her face, he said, "I missed you while you were in Los Angeles. I'm glad you're back. How did the shoot go?"

"It went well." She chewed on her lower lip and sighed. "Why didn't you call? Don't get me wrong. The emails were nice, but I would have loved hearing your voice." No accusation in her tone, only curiosity.

Still he flinched at the barb of defensiveness tip-toeing across his chest. Jasmine had warned him there would be setbacks. He'd fall back into old ways of viewing the world. "I knew you were going to be busy between work and family and didn't want to interrupt anything."

Sighing, he cupped a hand around her side and pulled her closer. Even to his own ears, his words smacked of excuse. While his counseling sessions were going well and he'd committed to taking the next step, putting one foot in front of the other wasn't easy. He knew she wanted more from him. More than anything, he wished he could give it. Someday. Hopefully before she got tired of waiting.

"Ever think we could be a real us and not just pretend? We are so good in bed. Why can't our emotions align?" She shifted, putting space between them—distance that felt like a chasm to him.

Nate rolled to his back and flung an arm across his eyes. "I am trying, but I'm not ready yet to think long-term." He cleared his throat and rolled back on his side to face her. "I started seeing Jasmine. I want to be the man who can love you with his whole heart." He brushed her cheek with his thumb, capturing the tear leaking from the corner of her eye. "Please don't cry. I can't tell you how sorry I am if I've hurt you. Can't we pretend a little while longer?" Dread singed him like a branding iron. He had no idea how long she'd continue to wait if he didn't reciprocate.

Lauren nodded, reaching up to smooth the worry lines from his eyes. "We can pretend for a while longer, but not forever. I think we have something special. I'd like to explore how special." She hitched a shoulder, but he saw the shadow of sadness.

"I have an idea," he said. "Isn't this the time when I'm supposed to make a romantic gesture?"

"What did you have in mind?" She skimmed a hand from his chest to his belly. "I think dinner and dancing is out. We'd have to get up and dressed." She waggled her eyebrows, "My plan is to stay here and cuddle."

"Cuddling works for what I have in mind." He rolled to his back and retrieved a book from the night stand. "I've been working on a song lyric for Zach and I'd like your opinion."

"Oh, that's so sweet." Her eyes shown with a tender light.

He loved the way her voice got all sugary and sappy. Warmed a deep place inside him. Sharing was less difficult each time they met. Maybe he could eventually get the hang of this closeness thing.

Nate pushed some pillows against the headboard and leaned back into their plump arms. "Zach's apparently smitten with a woman you know and wants a special song for her." He opened to a page he'd marked. "Here goes."

MY LOVE, MY HEART

You dropped into my life like a rocket,
a sassy sway in your hips
A smile that could stop a man dead in his tracks.
I thought I was doin' just fine, playing the field,

Then you walked into my life.
A raven-haired firecracker stole my heart
My soul mate walked through the door
A pint-sized beauty knocked me plum off my feet
I thought I was doin' just fine, playing the field,
Then you walked into my life.
She didn't want me, I was the wrong kind of man
Give me a chance, don't leave me
For you I will change, I will not disappoint
I thought I was doin' just fine, playing the field,
Then you walked into my life.
I don't know what hit me, but sure glad it did
You've made my life complete
You made me better, in ways I couldn't know
I thought I was doin' just fine, playing the field,
Then you walked into my life.
You've been hurt by love so many times in the past
And I'm just a simple Rodeo Man, that's who I am
Each of us had our own demons to slay, demons to slay
Before we could move on to find happiness
I thought I was doin' just fine, playing the field,
Then you walked into my life.
Please stay with me, grow old with me, joy and light of my soul
Walk with me down life's path, be my partner to the end.
I thought I was doin' just fine, playing the field,
I rejoice, you walked into my life.

"That's what I have so far. Zach's still working out the tune, but he said he could work with these beats."

"It's perfect for them." She flopped back on the pillow, her perky breast pointing to the ceiling. "Do you and Zach often collaborate on songs? You could be a professional."

"Aw, shucks ma'am." He felt heat spiraling up his cheeks. "Zach does sell some of our songs, so I guess we are professionals." He turned another page. "Here's a poem I've been working on. Part of my therapy." He shook his head. "There's a word in relation to myself I never thought I'd use." But he was glad it was out in the open.

"Sadly, there's a stigma attached to talking to a therapist, like there has to be something wrong with you if you do." Lauren squeezed his arm. "So we hide it from everyone, even the people who love us. Instead we should take pride in having the courage to take action." She tapped his journal. "Let's hear your poem."

SALVATION
Mind spinning
Caught in a carnival ride of emotions
Feeling sick
I grab for the railing
Seeking an anchor
Nothing.
Nothing to hold on to
Surrounded by
Fear — dark and suffocating
Engulfs me.
A soft touch
Gentle reassurance
Scent of wildflowers and fresh air
Flood into my weary soul
Her voice pulls me into the sunlight
I want to go, I long to go
But the fear, menacing and ugly
Blocks my path.
I will find a way around it
I will.
She is the life I want.

"Nate, ohhh," She waved her hand rapidly in front of her face and took several deep breaths. "Your words get to me every time. Have you ever thought about publishing them?"

"No, heaven forbid." The thought of putting his poems out there for others to see, had anxiety roaring back like a run-away train. "Real men in this part of the world don't write poetry unless it has something to do with cowboy life." He closed the book and set it back on the nightstand. "Enough of that. My poetry is for me." He brushed a kiss on her forehead. "And now you. It's private and personal."

"I respect that. I'm sure every single one of us has a deep secret we don't readily share."

"Oh, yeah. What's yours?"

"If I tell you, you have to promise you won't run screaming out of the room. The details aren't set in stone. I'm open to compromise."

"Okay." He braced for some wild, hair-brained adventure to match that free spirit personality of hers. She never made a secret of the fact she liked new experiences and seeing new places. It scared him to think she might take off someday when the whim hit her and leave him stranded. Another reason not to get too close.

"I want a large family. Five or six children and I want to stay home when they're little. Satisfy my nesting instincts and be there for my children, watch them grow, bake bread. Basically, I want to be an earth mother."

The expression on her face had him laughing out loud and enfolding her in his arms. "That's it? I thought you were going to tell me you were a black widow who killed off inadequate lovers."

"If that was my secret, you wouldn't have to worry." She patted his flat belly.

"Frankly, I was expecting to hear you wanted to hike Mt. Everest or live in the Amazon with natives for a year. Wouldn't having that many kids mean you'd have to stay in one place?" She'd definitely surprised him with her secret wish.

"We could always get a van and travel around the country like gypsies." She shrugged. "I'm not opposed to staying in one place, giving the family stability, if that's what you're driving at." She twisted so she could look at him. "That's why, until now, Ashley was the only person who knew my secret. Most people don't think what I want fits with who I am. I'm trusting you to believe me."

Nate felt his gut clench. Not as tightly as before he started therapy, but enough to know the thought of starting a family with Lauren unnerved him. Too much to lose. Yet, he also felt a faint stirring of excitement, like dawn peeking over the hills. If only he could reach out and grab it.

He bent forward and kissed her lips. "I'd like it if you'd stay the night." He shoved his uncertainty into the junk drawer in his mind. Hopefully he wouldn't find it for a while.

"I'd like that too." She returned his kiss.

He pulled her on top of him. "Now how about round two?

CHAPTER NINETEEN

"Hey, Todd, how're you doing?" Lauren draped an arm loosely across the boy's slight frame as she ushered him into her office. She felt a prickling in her scalp. He seemed more subdued today than usual. She'd hoped that summer vacation and getting away from the school environment would give him time to decompress.

"Okay."

Back to mumbling and clipped answers. "Where's your mom?"

"Busy. I took a cab. Can't wait to get my license." He sat in his usual spot and Lauren sat across from him.

"That's right. You have an important birthday coming up." She put as much enthusiasm in her voice as she could. "Excited?"

"Yeah, and my parent's sure won't mind getting me off their backs. Having to take me places messes up their schedules." Todd looked down and pressed his fingers into his forehead, shielding his eyes. "I think they liked it better when I spent most of my time in my room playing video games."

"How do you feel about that?" Lauren leaned forward slightly waiting for his answer. Unease tightened the back of her throat.

"Youth group has helped. I'm not the only one with parents who wish their child wasn't gay." His hands rested on knees that jittered up and down to the tempo of his restless feet.

Lauren reached over and covered one of his hands.

"Everyone shows affection differently. Just because your parents don't respond the way you expect them to, doesn't mean they don't care." She pushed the unease away. This was a routine, temporary setback. A young man adjusting to a new way of looking at his world.

"But it doesn't mean they do either," Todd said. She squeezed his hand and sat back.

"The only thing you can control is how you respond to them. Fair enough?"

"Yeah, I know. I've been practicing the positive self-talk we worked on—being gay is not a disease, it doesn't make me weird—and focusing on the list I made of the things that make me special…" He tossed his head to move a lock of hair out of his eyes. "But that doesn't change the fact I wish my parents liked me."

"What do they need to do to make you believe they care?"

"Stop being ashamed of me. My grandparents still don't know I'm gay. My parents try to hide my sexuality from their friends. They're more concerned about what other people think about them than what *I think*." He dropped his head, grasped handfuls of his hair and rasped out, "Why can't they say they love me?"

"I hear you. It's hurtful when people who should love us, don't seem to. Have you talked to them about what you're feeling?" He shook his head. "Would you like me to arrange a family session?" Todd was a great kid. She wanted to press on the hard knot forming in her chest. She knew if she could get them all talking, she could guide them toward a place of understanding.

"Maybe." He lifted one shoulder in a 'whatever' gesture.

"Have our visits helped you understand yourself better and why certain people react the way they do to someone who is not like them?"

Todd scowled and Lauren watched annoyance flick across his face before resignation set in. "Yeah, it helped."

"And?" The expression, 'pulling teeth,' came to mind.

"I'm learning to deal with the hurt, the anger, the guilt about who I am. When I am bullied, at least I understand the way they react is on them and not me," Todd said.

"So you're open to talking to your parents?"

He nodded.

"Good, I'll set up a time." She scribbled a note on her pad. "Tell me about the youth group."

"It's nice being with people who know who I am and don't make me feel like some kind of freak. For the first time in my life I'm with other kids who understand what my life is like."

"That's wonderful." She lifted her hand in a high five and he half-heartedly smacked her palm with his. "Didn't I also hear you're volunteering at the animal shelter?"

His face glowed with excitement. "I always wanted a dog, but my parents were afraid I wouldn't take care of it or would do something weird." Lauren watched his involuntary wince and her heart broke. "Now I know different. The dogs I take care of can count on me. That makes me feel good." His face brightened. "I also made the school's cross country team and summer practices have started."

"Now that we are on the subject of school…" Lauren watched him shrink into himself, "How do you feel about going back?" The poor kid was already starting to worry. She scribbled a note to add relaxation exercises to his routine.

He got up and walked behind the chair and gripped its back tightly. "If I never have to go back to that place, that'd be fine with me." He turned his back to her before Lauren could say anything. "Even if I could switch schools, bullies are everywhere. I guess I'm as prepared as I can be." He sat back down, his posture stiff and his hands fisted in his lap.

Lauren kept her face blank. "Is something going on you'd like to talk about?" Todd was not ready to return to this site of constant torment and fear. He was getting stronger, but it was too soon to test his fragile, new-found sense of self. She made a note to check with his parents about the possibility of sending him to one of the smaller charter schools where they might do a better job of monitoring bullying.

"A group of kids are making fun of me." He looked down at his feet avoiding eye contact. "It's annoying, but I can handle it."

"Are you sure? We can talk about some strategies for dealing with it."

He shook his head.

She had an idea that might help him feel more in control of events happening around him. "Do you know any other students who are being bullied?"

"Not personally, but I've seen a few."

"If you ever get the chance to help any of them, that's a great way to make new friends. You can make a difference, you know." Reaching out and helping would do wonders for his self-esteem and self-confidence.

His hands gripped his thighs. "I couldn't do that. They might come after me. I'm too scared." He hung his head and swiped at his eyes.

"That's okay. You need to take care of you first... No judgements about what you do or do not decide to do. One step at a time. I want you to keep journaling."

She stood up and walked him to the exit. She put a hand on his shoulder as he reached for the door knob. "You're going to get through this. Remember the videos you watched? Those people made it through high school. They're happy with their lives now, and you will be too. Hang in there. You're making great progress."

"I hope so." He walked out to meet his mom.

Lauren leaned against the door jamb. He was happier now than when she first saw him, so why did she sense storm clouds on the horizon? She sighed. Lately her instincts had been misfiring. She shook her head. Memories from the past haunting her? Todd had issues to deal with, but she saw positive changes in him. He was making great strides. All she needed was more time to work with him.

CHAPTER TWENTY

Nothing like shoe shopping with your besties to chase away the blahs. And the blahs had hit her hard the past few weeks. Her world was cockeyed on its axis. She hated the blahs. So not her. She picked up a sparkly pair of sandals, put them down. Picked up another pair with to-die-for styling, put them down. Sighed. She'd gotten a few emails from Nate since their incredible yoga date, but hadn't seen him. Yes, she pushed him to end the charade and become a real couple, but he'd seemed okay with the idea. Now this, back to hiding behind his protective wall. Was something wrong with her?

Crystal sucked in a breath. "Ash. *Those. Are. Perfect.* Wonder if they have them in my size."

Lauren glanced over. Ash had the same pair on her feet Lauren had just put down. Darn. Crystal was right. They *are* perfect. Man she *had* to shake off this funk.

Two sets of eyes under arched brows aimed straight at her.

"What?" The response too sharp. Lauren could see it in her friends' expressions. She held up her hands in surrender and dropped her chin to her chest. "Sorry," slipped out on a whisper. "I don't know what's wrong with me."

Ashley turned to the clerk. "Would you ring these up for me?" she said handing over her credit card.

Hands on hips, Ashley faced Lauren. "I think it's high time we had an early lunch and a *lot* of girl talk." She stabbed a perfectly manicured red fingernail at Lauren's chest. "We've given you enough time to sort through whatever is bothering you. Now it's time to spill."

"There's a nice, quiet, little restaurant right outside the mall." Crystal fished her phone from her purse. "I'm calling right now to make reservations. Ashley's right. You need to start taking some of the advice you dish out to your patients and start talking."

Lauren wasn't hungry, but maybe it would help to get things off her chest. Once they were seated at a small table and after they ordered, Lauren blurted out what was on her mind.

"I thought Nate and I were in a good place and our relationship was going somewhere. Now it's been two weeks and he's made no attempt to see me." Her confidence in her ability to read people and situations ticked down another notch. So this is what her patients who broke up with their boyfriends felt like. Pretty. Darn. Lousy. She'd never felt deeply about another man, so when they'd parted ways, she'd been sad but never lost her appetite, never felt aimless. Gaining empathy for what others experienced was a bitch.

"No, sweetie. Nate cares about you. I can tell." Ashley smiled up at the waiter as he slid their food in front of them.

"He probably has no idea how to handle what he's feeling for you," Crystal added sliding several shrimp and vegetables off the skewer and onto her plate.

"He'll come around. I can feel it." Ashley said, putting her hand over Lauren's.

"We've been seeing each other for six months. I've reached the point where, as my grandma used to say, '*he needs to piss or get off the pot.*' I told him we need to stop pretending we're a couple and start admitting that we actually care about each other." Lauren pushed her plate away. She appreciated her friends' support, but she was in the mood for action. If Nate couldn't love her with all his heart, then she had to stop pining for him and get on with her life. It was time to refocus on her career.

Crystals eyes went round and her mouth formed an 'oh.' "That explains a lot. Sue Ann called and said Nate's been working like a maniac the last few weeks." She sat back and crossed her arms. "He's always been obsessed with making the business successful, but lately you'd think demons were chasing him. Now we know what demon he's running from."

Ashley reached over and cupped Lauren's hand in hers. "The way he looks at you, there's love there, but I understand if you've had enough. No woman wants to be strung along. A man's got to make a decision at some point. I wish I had a magic wand so I could bring him to his senses. What are you going to do?"

"Before I leave for South Carolina, to spend the Fourth of July week with my family, we're going to talk."

****

Nate vaulted onto the bed of his truck and unhitched their bikes from the rack. The smooth play of muscles across his back and the stretch and pull in his thighs had Lauren's senses humming with longing. Even though she was trying to clear her schedule so she could leave on vacation, it was important to take this day off and spend time with Nate.

The day promised to be a hot one, but the cool, early morning air was refreshing. Birds whistled their songs, leaves whispered on the gentle breeze, and the lush green of trees and grass along the paved trails beckoned. At 9:00AM on a Friday they had the regional park to themselves. A good place to have that talk she intended to have with Nate. She hoped the peaceful setting would put him in a good frame of mind.

After two weeks, he'd finally called. As usual, when he disappeared from sight, he used work as his excuse, but today they planned to spend the entire day together. A bike ride this morning, a picnic at noon, movies this afternoon, followed by dinner and dancing tonight. Anticipation and anxiety had set up shop in her stomach since they'd made this date a few days ago. By the end of today, she'd know where they stood.

Nate rolled the bikes to a stop in front of her. Leaning

across them, he kissed her slowly, tenderly, before handing her bike over. They set off down the trail at a leisurely pace. For an hour they traveled in companionable silence, enjoying the terrain and the occasional challenge the switchbacks presented.

When they paused, they propped their bikes against a tree, hung their helmets from the handlebars, and sat on the gentle slope beside the trail. Lauren took a swig from her water bottle and handed it to Nate.

"It's beautiful here. So quiet. I forget what it's like without traffic and neighborhood noise." Nate handed the bottle back to Lauren who screwed on the cap and set it on the ground.

"That's one of the things I like best about my ranch. Nature is my symphony, but I can get into town whenever I want." He reclined onto his back, pillowing his head with his hands. "You're leaving Monday afternoon?"

"That's right. Thanks for taking the day off to be with me." She tucked her legs under her and cocked her head considering how to start the conversation they needed to have.

"I'm trying to be less tied to work and let others take some of the load. You'll be gone for two weeks?"

"Correct again. I saw Daphne and Ben in Los Angeles, but haven't seen the rest of my family since Christmas. Amazing how we let life get in the way and forget to make time for the things that matter most."

He sat back up, reached for her hand and placed it on his knee, covering it with his own. "I'm going to miss you."

Lauren scooted to face him. Time for the moment of truth. Nerves skittered down her spine. She took his face in her hands, staring intently into his eyes as though the answers were there. "How much will you miss me? Enough to make a commitment? It doesn't have to be a forever pledge, but maybe a willingness to think there might be a forever for us... I need you to talk to me."

Nate sat back, so her palms no longer framed his face,

but didn't release her hand. "I want to. Being with you feels more right than anything has in a long time." He guided her hand to his heart. "I'm falling for you, but I can't face the possibility of losing you."

"Anything can happen. There are no guarantees, but to have a full life, you have to risk the possibility of loss. How long will I have to wait before you know? We've been dating for six months. I know it's been pretend, but I thought something special was happening between us." A caged animal look marred his handsome features.

"I can't give you an answer. I'm working hard to get to the point where I can." He stood up and turned toward their bikes. "I think it's time to head back."

"Wait a minute. That's it? That's your answer?" She scrambled to her feet and grabbed his arm before he reached their bikes, turning him toward her. "You want to love me, but you can't? What exactly does that mean?" Frustration percolated like one of those old time coffee pots. Hot pops of heated water funneled to the bursting point.

"It means... *I. Don't. Know.* It means I care about you so much it's like a vulture pecking away at my innards. Pure torment and yet, I want you more than I've ever wanted anything in my life." The color had drained from his face. "Does that answer your question?"

She stood in stunned silence. Roughly he snatched his bike and set off down the path. Tension, tight as a python's hug, stretched between them as they returned to the parking lot. Tears pricked behind her eyelids. Pain and hurt pounded her chest like a madman at the door. She wouldn't cry in front of him. He could only give her what he could. Love couldn't be forced.

He went straight for his truck, dismounted and loaded his bike, then hers in the back. He leaned his butt against the side of his truck and crossed his arms. "I'm not much in the mood for a picnic or any of the other things we had planned. Let's say we call it a day."

She laid her hand on his arm. "I don't believe you can

think your way through this. Either you're ready to give love and accept it in return or you're not. If things change, come and find me." Her voice raspy with unshed tears.

Not a word was spoken on the drive to her house. There was nothing left to say. Once he unloaded her bike he folded her hands in his. "I'm obviously not able to give you what you need right now. I think it would be a good idea if we took a break for a while. Maybe saw other people."

The shock and pain must have been written across her face in bold colors because he continued.

"You deserve so much more than a broken man. I'm not sure even you—with your fierce determination to fix people—can make me better."

"You're serious? We're going our separate ways?" She pushed him away. "Tell me you don't already have someone else you want to start seeing."

"I don't. I told you, you're the only woman for me. Maybe you're the one who needs to do some thinking. Maybe your trip is a good thing. Gives us both some time to sort out where we stand and what we want."

He walked her bike to the door. "Look, I don't see this as an ending, only a short break. I do think that I'm going to get to the point where I can make the commitment you want. I just don't know how soon. I think it's only fair to give you the option of seeing other men. If you find love with someone else before I'm ready, then so be it."

So be it. That's how important she was to him? He planned to move on and get over her just like that? She walked inside and closed the door. Moving to the window, she watched him drive away. Right after she stowed the bike in the garage, her phone rang. Maybe it was Nate wanting to make amends.

CHAPTER TWENTY ONE

"Hi Lauren, sorry to bother you at home. I know you're trying to wrap things up so you can begin your vacation next week, but I have a call for you from Mrs. Westbrook. Can I forward it to you now?" Lauren recognized the voice of their receptionist. Disappointment sat like her grandma's fruitcake in her stomach, but she kept her tone light.

"Sure Emma. Other than packing, my schedule's clear. Did she say what she needed?" Odd to hear from her today since Lauren had an appointment with Todd and his mom on Monday before she left town that afternoon. A sense of unease filtered down her spine.

"No, but she sounded upset."

"Go ahead and put her through." She waited until she heard the click that the call had been transferred. "Hello, Mrs. Westbrook. How are you?"

"Todd's dead." The woman's voice devoid of emotion. No rise and fall. Flat. Eerie. "He committed suicide last night. We found him this morning."

"What?" The message hadn't yet found a place in Lauren's consciousness. Her knees buckled and she slid down the wall, bracing her back against it for support. "I'm so sorry for your loss... for everyone's loss. Todd was a wonderful kid." Her response sounded rote, even to her own ears yet she knew that she meant them.

"Why didn't you tell us his depression was getting worse?" The mother's voice rough with tears and pain, still layered with shock.

"When I saw him last week, he was happier than he's

been since I started seeing him. He was enjoying the summer activities with the youth group and spending more time at the animal shelter." Lauren pressed her fingers to her lips before she spoke again. "Did something happen?"

"Not that he said. He seemed his normal self." She paused and Lauren heard her draw in a breath. "He had cross country practice yesterday." The mother's voice hitched in anguish. "Why didn't you make us understand how bad it was for him? How much he was being bullied? Made sure we transferred him to that other school?"

Had she worked hard enough to make the situation clear? To get the Westbrooks to act? She failed them, like she'd failed Patsy so many years ago. Lauren felt the numbness of shock building around the edges—pressing in like the complete lack of light. Todd, her heart shouted, a sweet kid with so much life ahead of him.

"Mrs. Westbrook, you made the decisions you thought were in Todd's best interests. There was no guarantee things would have been different elsewhere. Teens are very good at hiding their feelings from everyone. It's unlikely he would have let you see how troubled he was."

"But I'm his mother. *I should have known.*"

Lauren was the one who should have known. She should have seen through Todd's mask. "Don't blame yourself for what happened. Please feel free to reach out to me at any time if you need to talk. Even though I'm going to be away for a while, my office can always reach me. I'm available whenever you want to talk."

"I don't blame myself. It's the school that let this happen and you. You let this happen." Her voice vibrated with anger. "We should sue you and the school for negligence."

The threat of a lawsuit should have generated panic, but the concept couldn't penetrate the void inside. Lauren kept her voice calm, reassuring, reasonable. The woman needed comfort. "Mrs. Westbrook, I urge you to talk to a grief counselor. Right now all of this is hitting you hard and fast. Give yourself time to process and to say goodbye to your son."

"That's easy for you to say. You don't have children. You've never experienced how I feel."

The phone disconnected. Rationally, she knew the woman needed an outlet for her pain and was lashing out at the nearest targets. Emotionally, Lauren felt the blame hit its target. Was Mrs. Westbrook right? Was Todd's death on her? She couldn't think about that now. Todd—the boy who loved video games and animals, bright with a dry sense of humor that caught a person unaware. All he'd wanted in life was to be accepted. It hit her that she would never see him again. He had so much promise. His death didn't make sense. His last sad smile would be forever imprinted on her brain.

Easing to a standing position she walked over to the French doors to let the dogs in before deflating onto the sofa. She tossed her cell phone on the coffee table and sank back resting her head on the back of the sofa. One of the dogs nuzzled her hand pushing it onto its head. Without thought she rubbed its silky fur taking small comfort in its warmth and companionship.

Detachment, like an outer body experience, engulfed her. As though caught in a dream, she couldn't process the news of Todd's death. Was this how Nate felt? No, he couldn't have. He hadn't missed anything. He had done everything he could for Sharon. But sometimes everything wasn't enough.

Searing pain would come later. She knew that from working with clients, but at the moment every bit of energy she possessed had evaporated. Actions she should take pounded on the shell she was. She ignored them. Calling Jasmine could wait. Packing for her trip could wait. Cancelling her other Monday morning appointments could wait… or should she cancel them? She had a responsibility to fulfill. Questions swirled like a dust devil, choking in its intensity. She wanted to gasp for air, but sat inert. She couldn't think about any of this now. Her mind refused to process Todd's death. She closed her eyes. Her fingers dug into her scalp and moved in circular motions.

She felt empty. Nothing left inside. Nothing for her. Nothing for her family and friends. Nothing for her clients. Nothing even for Nate. Hollow. The first stage of grief, denial, giving her psyche time to adjust to the loss. Deal with the pain in small increments.

Sighing, she lifted herself away from the sofa and picked up the phone. She told Jasmine what had happened, that she would be extending her vacation and, yes, they would talk soon about coping with this loss. Her next call was to Ashley.

****

Nate's hand tingled as the powerful miter saw sliced through the 2x4 lumber used to make the top and bottom railings for the gazebo. Zach had finally asked Ashley to marry him, she'd accepted, and their mom wanted the gazebo built for the wedding. She'd marched them all straight home from church and put them to work. His dad held the wood in place on the saw horses so each cut followed the carefully measured angles marked on the wood. Electric drills whirred while Zach and Josh worked on their piece of the project. The smell of sawdust permeated the air.

He needed this time to think. The last two days had been hell. The scene at the park with Lauren had run in a constant loop in his head. Over and over. Had he screwed everything up? Made the worst mistake of his life? He loved Lauren. He'd known for a while. Did he really need more time before he could drop the charade and make a commitment to her? She was everything he wanted. Jasmine was right. He needed to do what his heart urged him to do and trust that he and Lauren could handle the times uncertainty and fear reared its ugly head.

"Your mama does like her gingerbread look," Jack said examining one of the curlicue pieces of wood destined to grace the structure. "Thank heavens we don't have to paint the dang thing white. That would have been a pain in the butt to keep up." Nate welcomed the interruption. He was getting nowhere with his thoughts.

"Stop grousing, Dad. You know if Mom wanted it white, we'd all be going, *'yes ma'am, what color white do you prefer?'*" Nate stopped and lifted his hat, swiping his arm across his forehead.

"You boys about ready for a break?" Gloria June walked across the lawn carrying a tray of lemonade and cookies.

"Thanks Mom, this hits the spot." Nate lifted a glass from the tray along with a cookie.

"You boys are making nice progress. Going to have that railing in place today and the roof tomorrow?"

"That we are." Jack kissed his wife on the cheek and followed her into the house.

Nate joined his brothers and lowered himself into one of the lawn chairs, stretching his legs out in front of him. "I thought for sure Ashley would be here supervising," he said.

"Something came up and she's taking Lauren to the airport today," Zach replied. "Otherwise, I'm sure she would be."

"Oh," was all Nate could force out. Guilt clung to him like plastic wrap, suffocating and tight.

Both Zach and Josh eyed their brother. "What'd you do this time?" Zach asked.

"Uh… Well…"

"Come on, rip that Band-Aid off," Josh prodded.

"We'd planned to spend all day Friday together. It started off great with a bike ride, but then Lauren wanted to know, and I quote, 'am I willing to make a commitment to us as a couple. Be willing to think there might be a forever for us.' What's a man supposed to say to that?"

Zach looked heavenward and then at Nate. "You're shitting me, right?"

"And what *did you say?*" Josh shook his head. "I'm supposed to be the dunderheaded brother, and *even I know*, when a woman like Lauren asks that question, the answer is, *'yes, I'll make a commitment to you, honey. Right now, this minute.'*—

even if you're not quite ready. Man up and do it."

"I sorta said yes." Nate scowled, but knew in his heart, his brothers were right. He'd really bungled this one. He cringed. "I might have suggested we need a break from each other, possibly see other people." He grimaced, then brightened. "But I did tell her I thought commitment was a real possibility in the future." He hunched forward, "I just don't know when."

Zach reached over and smacked his brother on the back of his head. "Mush for brains. You know you're crazy about her. If she does give you the proverbial boot—which I might add it sounds like you royally deserve—how happy will you be without her in your life? Are you ready to have her be in the arms of another man?"

Nate saw red. The veil lifted. If another man touched her, he'd strangle him with his bare hands. Damn. "You're right. As soon as Sue Ann's back from vacation so we're not short-handed at the clinic, I'm on my way to South Carolina. Sounds like I may need to eat a whole truckload of humble pie."

"No guessing about it, big bro," Zach said. "You need to haul ass there as soon as possible and tell that woman whatever she needs to hear to take you back."

CHAPTER TWENTY TWO

Lauren padded down the stairs in yoga pants and crop top, her bare feet silent on the wooden treads. She'd wanted to stay in bed, hold on to the nothingness for a while longer, but if she didn't get up, her mom would come looking for her. Her parents knew something was wrong when she arrived a day early and planned to stay for a month. Yesterday they'd given her space. Today, probably not.

The smell of fresh coffee drew her through the sunny dining room and into the kitchen. Her mom, Missy to friends and Marilyn to everyone else, fussed over a pot on the stove.

"The coffee smells amazing but… is that lavender?" Her mother nodded. Lauren closed her eyes and inhaled deeply. "It smells heavenly." Hopefully its purported healing properties would help lift the depression bearing down on her mind like a huge stone boulder she couldn't budge.

Everything about being home brought solace to her weary soul. She hadn't talked about her change in demeanor, but her mother's radar was up and active. Pretty soon she'd have to share what had happened. Not yet.

She wrapped her arms around her mother's slender waist and rested her chin on her shoulder, peeking over to examine this latest project. "What *are* you doing?"

"Making lavender soap." Her mother continued to stir the concoction in the double boiler. "I saw bars of this soap in a gift shop and thought they'd make great Christmas gifts." She glanced at her daughter, a frugal housewife expression on her aging beauty-queen face. "But at $8 each, I decided to try making them myself before shelling out the cash."

"Great idea," Lauren said. She picked up a muffin tin lined with paper cups and filled with a creamy-looking, pale lavender mixture that reminded her of soft candle wax. "Pretty." She put the tin back on the counter. If she could pretend life was normal, she might be able to forget the sadness swirling around her like a whirlpool slowly sucking her toward the center.

"Those are about ready to unmold. I tried a goat's milk recipe with that batch. The one I'm working on now will have oatmeal mixed in with the lavender buds, like a scrub."

Lauren poured herself coffee, added cream and sweetener, and leaned a hip against the counter.

"Do you want some breakfast?" her mother asked looking at her like she was one of the wounded birds Lauren had brought home as a child.

"I'm not very hungry. I plan to do yoga in the sunroom first." Lauren walked over to the pantry and rummaged around until she found an energy bar to tide her over.

"You know we love to have you, but I was surprised you decided to stay for an entire month. You usually don't want to be away from work that long. Is something wrong, dear?"

Lauren busied herself straightening kitchen towels on the rack wondering how long she could stall her mother. Experience taught her—not very.

Missy removed her apron and, with her hand on her hip, faced her daughter. "You don't have to talk about it if you're not ready, but *I'm here* when you are."

A tear trickled down Lauren's cheek and she took a fortifying sip of coffee. "I've had a crappy…" Her hand covered her mouth and she swallowed hard. "That's an understatement. Crappy doesn't begin to describe the last few days."

With her mom's arm across her back, Lauren let her guide her out to the sunroom where they sat on the small sofa. Resting her head against her mother's chest and nurturing arms wrapped around her, Lauren felt the comfort she always did in her mother's embrace. Light poured in from the many windows. Lauren could see through the French doors to the deck and lush gardens beyond. *Home is where one comes to heal.*

"Tell me what happened." Missy's voice, soft as warm honey, flowed into the broken parts of Lauren's spirit.

"One of my clients committed suicide—a young teenager with his whole life in front of him." Lauren's voice teetered on unshed tears. "I tried, but couldn't help him see his life was worth living."

"Oh honey, I'm so sorry. You must be devastated." Her mother's arms tightened around Lauren.

"Devastated? At the moment I don't know what I feel. Empty. Lost. Guilty. I should have sensed something was wrong. Seen how fragile he still was." She squeezed her mom a little tighter. "Mom it hurts so much." She felt her mom's shirt grow damp against her cheek. Tears were good, part of embracing the grief. By accepting the pain, grief would boil through her until it evaporated. People who didn't, like Nate, allowed grief to simmer indefinitely giving it the power to trap their emotions in an insulated bubble. "Mom, do you think I made a mistake by becoming a psychologist? Am I cut out for this work?"

"Lauren." Her mother's hand stroked her hair, her voice pouring out empathy for her daughter's pain. "You're the child who brought home every stray, who made time to visit friends, family—and the occasional stranger—in the hospital, listened to people and took on their problems as your own. You care."

"But is that enough?" Was caring and empathy enough if the end result was failure?

"Sweetheart, I do believe you were born to help people get through tough times. Unfortunately, not everyone can be helped." Missy patted her daughter's back. "Yes, I believe you made the right career choice."

"Thanks Mom. My plan is to take a month off to decompress and reevaluate my life." She sat up, sadness etched on her classic features. "As if losing my client wasn't enough, Nate and I decided to take a break in our relationship. Basically, my life is a mess."

"I'm glad you're taking some time off to take care of yourself." Missy shifted Lauren's head on to her shoulder and patted her back. "While you know your family would move heaven and earth to help you, I hope you'll talk to someone with the skills to help you cope with everything."

Lauren listened to the soft vibrations of her mother's voice, the steady beat of her heart, and relaxed against her. A tissue was pressed into her hand. How did mothers always know what their children needed?

"Jasmine emailed earlier today and we've set a time to talk on the phone this afternoon." Lauren sat up and rested her hands on her mom's knees. "If it's alright with you, I'd like to invite her to fly out and join us for the long weekend."

"Of course you can. We've got plenty of room." She patted her daughter's arm and stood up. "You go ahead and do your yoga while I clean up the kitchen. Then we can have breakfast together, and you can tell me what this business is with you and Nate."

****

After her call with Jasmine that afternoon—which *had* been calming—followed by the call to the practice's liability company—*not* so calming and one more worry to pile on her plate—Lauren wandered down to the end of their street to sit on the stone bench and stare out over the ocean. The raucous squawk of seagulls and the briny scent of the salt marsh filled the air.

She pulled out the journal she'd brought with her, and obeyed Jasmine's suggestion to record her thoughts—chaotic though they were, she had to try and create some kind of order. That sounded like Nate talking in her head. She was beginning to understand a lot of things now. Nate's desire for order. Why her clients questioned whether journaling would help them make sense of whatever turmoil they were going through. The futility of thinking she could find solutions to all problems. Her thoughts tumbled round and round like clothes in a dryer.

What *did* she feel? Like a big bowl of sadness topped with a huge dollop of guilt and a large ladle of emptiness that seeped into every nook and cranny—a hot fudge sundae of misery. She held out her hands, wiggled her fingers. Stretched her feet in front of her and flexed them. Her body parts seemed to be in good working order. How could that be when everything inside was blank? Blank and cold and confusing. She wasn't ready for self-analysis yet. She needed a project. Something to keep her hands busy until her mind could focus again. After making a few quick notes in her journal, she trudged home hoping to find something to occupy her hands and her mind.

****

The next day, Lauren paused for a moment to admire the antebellum architecture of her father's insurance office in downtown Charleston. She'd promised to have lunch with him. That was one of the things she and Nate had in common—she didn't break promises. She wasn't hungry. She didn't particularly want company, but here she was. Lauren dug deep to summon the cheerful, confident attitude everyone expected from her. Her dad didn't deserve to have the dark cloud hanging over her head inflicted on him. She adjusted the purse strap on her shoulder and forced herself up the walkway.

"Hi Lorraine, is Dad ready?" Thankfully modeling had given her lots of practice at fake smiling.

The receptionist returned Lauren's smile. "He is, but your brother expects a hello before you take off. Just head on up."

Lauren walked past the well-appointed waiting area and through the double doors into the open hallway. On one side was the downstairs conference room and on the other the clerks cubicles. She ascended the stairs and entered a broad hallway lined with the partners' offices. She stepped into her brother's office.

He got up from his desk as she entered the room and swamped her in a crushing bear hug. "It's good to see you, little sis. Sorry I can't join you and dad for lunch, but someone has to keep the place humming." He held her at arm's length and perched on the edge of the desk.

"It's good to see you too," Lauren said. "How are Cheryl and the kids?"

"Kids are growing like weeds and now that they are all in school, Cheryl is thrilled to be back to teaching full time. Everyone is looking forward to seeing you this weekend."

"I heard you were in town." A familiar deep voice hailed her from the doorway.

Lauren turned. Connor, her first love. He waited, blue eyes alight with mischief, a wide grin on his chiseled face, arms open, inviting her to walk in to them. She obliged, welcoming the reminder of a more innocent time when the biggest decision was what to wear to the Prom. She wished she could chuck the guilt and sadness weighing her down and be that carefree girl again. So much for the strength of character she'd prided herself on. First sign of trouble and she wanted nothing more than to crawl in a hole. Gave her a new perspective on Nate's strength. He'd managed to find a way to keep going.

"Dad told me you'd joined the agency," Lauren said. "Who would have thought, high school jock and local playboy would turn into a staid insurance salesman." She kissed his cheek and stepped away. "How in the world have you managed to stay single this long?"

"Been keeping track?" She could almost see the glints reflecting off his teeth like a comic book hero. "And who said I was staid?" He narrowed his eyes in mock offense.

"No one in the female population." Maybe she could reignite the flame she once shared with Connor and he could help her forget about Nate. Hurt and despondency weighed her down like a lead vest in the dentist's office. At present, she was too numb to consider any possibility except the comfort of a friend.

Lauren returned to her brother and gave him a kiss and a hug. "I'll see you in a few days." She tucked her arm in Connor's. "I'll walk you to your office."

"I could ask you the same question…" he said putting his hand over hers.

She arched her brow. After all these years was Connor still carrying a torch for her? A tiny glow, a flicker really, gained a toehold in her frozen interior. Could this be a sign that San Antonio wasn't where she belonged and South Carolina was? She wasn't sure of anything anymore – except she wasn't in the proper state of mind to make a decision.

"How'd you manage to stay single?" Connor asked.

"Been keeping track?" she asked. It felt good to chuckle and flirt with a good-looking man. Restorative. Distracting. No matter how brief the respite.

"Since you're single, and I'm single, and the weather promises to hold, would you like to go paddle boarding with me next week?"

Her fingers traced the letters of his name on the engraved sign on his door. "That sounds like fun. Why not?" And why not indeed? Nate had made his feelings clear. A serious relationship was not in his immediate future—and maybe never. Spending time with Connor out on the water might help clear her mind.

He smiled again. "*Why not*, wasn't the reaction I hoped for, but it's a start."

They exchanged phone numbers, then she walked to her father's door and tapped.

"Come in," he called. He held up a finger and pointed to the phone as she entered. She took a moment to reacquaint herself with her dad's masculine space. Mahogany paneling lined the walls and ceiling. Cove molding created an intricate pattern of rectangles on the ceiling set with recessed lighting. Sunlight slanted across the plush, oriental rug and dignified, leather wing chairs waited for visitors.

She moved to one of the floor to ceiling bookcases and ran her finger along the titles. Smiling, she pulled out one of the children's books she had so loved as a young girl. This had been one of her favorite places to come after school. She turned toward the window seat and visions of a lanky ten-year-old curled up there with a book danced in her head.

Her father walked over and engulfed her in a '*that's my little girl*' hug. "I can still see you there with your head bent over a book… or more often, you and Ashley hatching some plot." He walked over to a valet stand in the corner and slipped on his jacket. "Ready to go, cupcake?"

"With the handsomest man in town? You bet."

Once they were out on the sidewalk, he turned toward the harbor. He placed her hand in the crook of his elbow and covered it with his. "It's so good to see you again. It's been too long. We'll have to make a point of getting together more often."

"You'll be out for Ashley's wedding and I'll be back for Christmas again. We'll probably get sick of each other."

"I doubt that, and we want to be there for you when you need us."

"Dad, you've never been any good at beating around the bush, so just say what you have to say." She gently nudged him sideways as they walked.

"Your mom tells me you've hit a rough patch. As your dad, there's nothing I want more than to kiss that boo-boo, put a Band-Aid on it, and make everything better. Shame grown up life can't be that simple."

"Life does get complicated." She plucked a leaf off a shrub as they passed, smoothing it between her fingers. "I assume mom told you that I lost a client to suicide?"

"She did. Honey, I am so sorry you have to deal with this."

"Me too. That's why I extended my trip—to give myself space and time to cope."

"You know you can stay as long as you like."

"I appreciate the offer." She dropped the leaf and watched it float to the ground. "I'm giving myself a month, then I'm back to San Antonio to put my life back together or pack up and come home. I've always been so sure I made the right choices. Now I don't know. Maybe I'm not meant to be a therapist. I've been thinking I could fall back on modeling until I decide."

"Sweetheart, I'm pretty sure you know what you're saying is grief talking." He slipped an arm across her shoulder and leaned his head close to hers. "You're good at what you do. You have a natural empathy and uncanny sense for what people need. Don't make any hasty decisions." He squeezed her hand and opened the door to the restaurant.

CHAPTER TWENTY THREE

They sat in the sunroom facing each other on the small sofa, each cradling a mug of coffee in their hands.

"Your parent's home is beautiful." Jasmine sat with her feet curled under her. "I've never been to the Charleston area so this is a treat."

"I'm so glad you could come. I'm sure you probably had other plans."

"Other than a picnic with Randy—who needs a reminder that my life *is not arranged* for his convenience—I'd planned to catch up on paperwork. This is a nice break." She patted Lauren's knee who was sitting cross-legged pressing a pillow to her chest.

Guilt trickled down Lauren's throat. Her absence meant more work for everyone else. "I suppose you want to hear how I'm doing?" Lauren squeezed the pillow tighter.

"I know that you know, but I'll add this disclaimer anyway—in the grieving process, a week is a very short time. No expectations." Jasmine scooted into the corner of the sofa, propped her elbow on the armrest and stretched the other along the back of the sofa. "Would you like to talk about what you've experienced so far?"

Tight-lipped, Lauren nodded. "If my voice cracks, forgive me. The emotions are so raw, yet."

"Understandable." Jasmine sipped her coffee. "I'm here to listen not only as a professional, but as your friend."

"I feel a little more clear-headed than when I arrived. It's helped to have family around and busy-work projects to keep me from staying in my head." Lauren plucked at the pillow.

Where were the words she needed to express what she felt? She may have a clearer head, but was far from precise. Was this how her clients felt? Maybe she wasn't as good as she thought at internalizing what people were going through. "If I'd remained in San Antonio trying to act like nothing had changed, I would have gnawed on the situation like a bone," Lauren said.

"I'm glad you took time off to give yourself space. How has the grief affected you so far?"

"Mild depression, but I'm determined I won't try to suppress it. I'm tired but I force myself out of bed every day. Luckily my mom has plenty of projects." Lauren's lips curved in a sad little smile. "I can't face the reality that Todd is gone. A part of me still expects to see him when I return." She set her now cold coffee on the end table. "What I struggle with most is that I'm questioning my ability as a therapist. I keep running the sessions I had with Todd through my mind and can't help wondering if I did everything I could for him. Did he say something I should have picked up on?" Lifting the guilt was like trying to heft a 500 pound weight.

Jasmine stretched forward, placed her hands on Lauren's shoulders and touched foreheads. "Sometime during most mental health professional's career, one of their clients will commit suicide. In fact statistics put that number at about 50 percent." She sat up and faced Lauren. "Even though you question yourself now, I've looked over your case notes and can tell you that you did everything you could, but I think it would help you if we reviewed each session you had with Todd. I brought your notes with me." She opened her laptop and clicked on a file.

Lauren had been dreading this moment. She wasn't sure she had the strength or clarity to scrutinize her work. She'd seen Todd at least once a week for the past five months. That was a lot to relive, a lot to process, and a lot to question. The thought terrified her. Had she been hiding behind false confidence all these years and now her true self was emerging? She closed her eyes and braced herself. "Okay, let's do it."

They spent the better part of three hours poring over Lauren's notes. Missy brought in sandwiches and quietly retreated. Sometime during the long hours, Lauren realized the pressure on her chest eased and the sick feeling in her stomach lessened—not much but a little. Jasmine was right. She did need to face the work she had done head on if she ever hoped to get past this.

Jasmine closed her laptop and set it on the coffee table. "Any questions about what we've reviewed?"

Lauren blew out a long breath and felt the first glimmer of light in the dark recesses of her grief. She had a long way to go, but reviewing everything she'd done, put a miniscule dent in her doubts. "No questions, but you've given me a lot to think about."

"I can almost guarantee that questions will come. Write them down and we'll go over them—any time day or night." Jasmine folded her hands together in her lap and gazed out the window for a moment deep in thought. Finally she turned back to Lauren. "We have to accept that despite our best efforts, clients don't always follow our advice and hurt themselves. It's painful, but there is only so much we can do."

"I suppose it was naïve of me to think that because the training for this career came easy and I excelled at it, that the career itself would be easy." Lauren wanted to kick herself for the attitude she'd had, but she was going to change. Yes, she should continue to trust her instincts, but she needed to temper that with a big dose of reality.

"Since none of us can predict the future, we can't know everything that will happen. People make choices we can't foresee, based on reasons they hide from us," Jasmine said. She sat back and brushed a strand of hair off Lauren's forehead. "Your natural empathy is part of what makes you such a great therapist, but it also deepens the pain. With time, you'll heal, but you'll never forget. You'll take this experience with you into everything you do moving forward. It will color the way you look at the world and the people you help. What you learn in the next weeks and months will make you better at what you do."

Lauren stood up and Jasmine followed suit. "Thank you. I couldn't get through this without your support." She gripped her in a tight hug. "I'm glad you're staying for a few days."

Jasmine slipped her arm around Lauren's waist and propelled her toward the kitchen. "Todd's suicide is not your fault. Accepting that fact won't come easy, but at some point you will." Jasmine stood up. "I think it's time you showed me a few of the sights. No pressure, but let's spend a quiet day outside."

****

Connor had followed up on his invite to go paddle boarding with him. Now that she was on the dock practicing the basic moves, her early morning inertia floated away like the haze on the bayou. As a psychologist she understood the impact grief had, but that did nothing to minimize the pervasive lack of motivation that had plagued her the past two weeks. Jasmine's visit, and being surrounded by family, helped provide relief. She longed to get her joie de vivre back.

Bless his heart, Connor had arrived on her doorstep with coffee and blueberry scone in hand, a warm smile on his face, and friendship in his arms which he wrapped around her like a comfy shawl, soft, inviting, and familiar. Unfortunately, that's all she felt—friendship—but maybe that would blossom into something more serious given time.

"I think you've got the hang of it so let's get in the water." Connor gently slipped her SUP—short for 'stand up paddleboard'—in the water and steadied it. "Sit here." He patted the dock. "Swing your feet onto the board and then place one on each side of the hand well. Use your paddle for balance and stand up."

"I'm just supposed to stand up? Won't it tip?" She looked up at him uncertainty in her eyes. Where had her sense of adventure run off to? Three weeks ago, before Todd, she would have been eager for this new experience.

"Nope. All you have to do is maintain an even weight distribution on both feet. Remember, think of your feet as triangles—heel is one point and the pads behind your big and little toes are the other two points—you're going to press that triangle into the board. Nice wide stance."

"Okay." She held her breath and stood, wobbling a little, but remained standing.

"Paddle out a few yards while I get on my board."

"I'm doing it. I'm doing it." She gently shifted her hips back and forth, getting a feel for the movement of the board under her. Maybe some of her old self had survived.

"Whoa, now. Don't get too excited," Connor said.

"This is grrreeeaaat." She elongated the word. "Where to?" The water calmed her, like meditation, and gave her mind a rest.

"Up the creek," his chuckle teased out her chuckle, "but not without a paddle."

Lauren rolled her eyes and groaned, enjoying a respite from the gloom dampening her spirits.

They spent the next two hours getting a fantastic core workout and soaking in the tranquil waterway. It felt wonderful to be out and about. Dolphins glided by their backs barely breaking the surface, pelicans skimmed the water, and white egrets waded in the marsh grasses. Water lapped gently against their boards as their paddles pushed them forward. The pungent smell of the river marshes tickled her nose.

Back at the dock, Lauren helped Connor load the boards into the back of his truck. She was comfortably tired and surprisingly content. "Thank you for today. I don't' feel as stressed."

"I thought it might help. Getting out on the water and building up a sweat while communing with nature always improves my mood." I heard about your client. I'm sorry. Since you've never been a stressed out person, I assume that's the cause?"

Everything inside her deflated like an old tire. Her temporary reprieve from melancholy wandered off into the surrounding bayou. "I haven't been able to get my mojo back." Lauren looked out over the water and then back at Connor. "Again, thanks for today. Since we were kids, you've had a knack for knowing what I needed." She saw the gleam in his eyes and inwardly winced at the next words out of his mouth.

"Any chance we could repeat history? That is if you aren't currently seeing someone." His pose, leaning against the side of the truck looked casual, but she read the underlying vulnerability in his body language.

"Yes and no about seeing someone…" She sighed. "It's complicated. I was—am—serious about someone, but have no idea where our relationship is headed. At the moment, I can't think beyond tomorrow." She ran a hand down his arm and looked into his eyes, a sad smile on her lips. "I have to be honest. I don't know that I feel the same way about you that I did a decade ago. I'm not the same woman I was in high school. I want us to be friends, but doubt there will ever be more between us."

"I understand. Sparks fly or they don't." He wrapped her in a loose embrace. "You never forget your first love," Connor said. "There will always be a warm spot in my heart for you, but like the old saying, going home is never what you thought it would be. Friends it is." He stuck out his hand, they shook, and then he kissed her lightly on the forehead.

Disappointment circled her. Nate was the direction her heart pointed. Until they sorted out where they stood, her love life was on hold. Nate had called every day since she'd been here to find out how she was. He must care about her, but still not one word about the possibility of long-term. Why couldn't she fall for a man who was crazy about her and came without baggage? She supposed that would be too simple.

CHAPTER TWENTY FOUR

Nate climbed into his rental car and punched the address Lauren had given him into the navigation system. It had taken him two weeks to get work squared away so he could join her in South Carolina. When he'd called after the plane landed, she'd said she would see him, but he had no idea what kind of reception he'd get. He'd see her first, and then settle into his hotel—or head back home his life in tatters. If he couldn't make things right with Lauren, maybe he should become a monk and give up on his dream of home and family. He blew out a breath, nerves zinging like angry wasps.

Even though he'd made a point of talking to her daily over the last two weeks—and he'd told her he wanted to visit, if she'd have him—she'd been surprised he'd actually come. He'd heard it in her tone. Her surprise was not unexpected. He'd stepped outside his comfort zone and let instinct take over. Fear of getting hurt wasn't going to control his life any longer. Besides, he needed to see her. To see for himself that she hadn't fallen into the same quagmire he had.

Ashley told him about Lauren's client's suicide and her need to get away for a while. He'd wanted to hop on the first plane after he heard the news, but remembered the numbness of the first few weeks of grief. In the early stages, the mind needed that numbness to come to terms with the loss. He understood, probably better than anyone around her, what she was going through. This was not the time for declarations of love, but he hoped by the end of the week, she would understand how important she was to him. That he wanted her in his life—long-term. His heart beat faster and a sheen of sweat dampened his forehead. His jaw clamped tight. No more running. No more hiding. He was going after what he wanted.

He put the car in gear and pulled away from the airport angling toward the expressway skirting North Charleston that would drop him in the Mt. Pleasant suburb. Along the way he passed heavily wooded sections and crossed bridges spanning rivers and marsh land. Light industrial complexes carved out space here and there. In town he passed modern apartment and condo structures and a quaint, historic downtown district before turning into a residential area filled with pure, old South charm and grace.

Parking in the gravel area in front of the house, he rested his arms on the steering wheel. He peered up at the two story antebellum home that in this neighborhood probably passed for modest. He sat in his car for a few minutes wondering what the heck he could say to her. *Hi, honey, I'm home? Take me, I'm yours? Kick me because I'm dumber than dirt? Forgive me for even thinking about letting the best thing that ever happened to me go?* Yup, that last one might be the best place to start, combined with as much groveling as it took to get the job done. He wanted to go back in time before that disastrous day in the park. Pretend it never happened. Not possible. That day *had* happened. He'd hurt her badly and then her client's death had knocked her world sideways.

He opened the car door and stood. The front door to the house swung wide and Lauren stepped out. Even from this distance, he could see she'd lost weight since he'd last seen her. A melancholy replaced her usual confident, nurturing self. His chest tightened in empathy.

They met halfway. Despite the weariness in her eyes and the momentary hesitation, she still wanted to come to him. Even after the way they'd parted and the tragedy she'd suffered. Joy surged in him like a refreshing dip in the pool. Maybe they *could* figure out how to get to forever. It was his turn to be patient, to be there for her. His arms folded around her. Man, it felt good to have her back in his embrace. He kissed her temple and rested his chin on the top of her head.

"If I could take your pain away, I gladly would," he said. Her arms tighten around him. She pressed closer, as though seeking shelter from life's storms. He wanted to provide that shelter. His protective instincts kicked in to high gear. Shifting her back just far enough for his hands to frame her face, he kissed her lightly on the lips, lingering, wanting to share his strength with her. "I'm here for you, and will be here for as long as you need me. I planned to stay a week, but will stay longer if you want me to."

"Can you take that much time off? I know how much rides on the success of your practice."

There was no reproach in her voice, only acceptance that his work was part of who he was. "My partners can handle it. The practice will survive fine if I'm away for a while."

Her hand skimmed down the stubble on his cheek. He felt the whiskers pull slightly. Her clear, penetrating gaze pierced him—her sensitivity seemed to see into his darkest places. Hopefully she saw the beam of light penetrating the darkness.

"I'm glad you came. I wasn't sure I would be, but I am. There's something different about you..." She shrugged. "Come on inside. I want you to meet my family." Grasping his hand, she started to lead him up the walk, stopped, turned to him and held up one finger. "I should warn you, when mom heard you were coming, she phoned my brother and sister and invited them over."

He brought her hand to his lips. She was so darn cute when she was trying to protect him. "Honey, if I were the kind of man who was intimidated by family, I would have turned into a hermit years ago." He smiled at the relief on her face. "Bring 'em on. I'm ready."

For a minute, with the cacophony of sounds that greeted him when he stepped through the door, he thought he'd wandered into a hen house. A gaggle of children shrieking with laughter, their feet pounding the hardwood floors, stampeded like wild horses. A pack of adults circled him, slapping his back or pumping his arm. Maybe he'd been a bit premature in his assessment.

Finally, an older, slightly shorter version of Lauren, moved in front of him, facing the onslaught, staring them into submission as only a mother and wife could. Once they'd backed politely away, she turned to him.

"Hi, I'm Missy, Lauren's mom. This is Sam, her father." She pointed to a tall, distinguished man with silver hair and sparkling blue eyes.

"We'll sort out all the children later, but this is Lauren's brother, Adam, and his wife, Cheryl." A dark-haired man, who looked like he would be a great tennis player, and a slim brunette, who looked like she'd stepped out of a charm-school ad, extended their hands.

"And this is Lauren's sister, Tammy, and her husband, Evan." A blonde pixie hauled him in for a quick hug while a man who might have played basketball in college clamped his hand in a tight grip. Didn't look like shyness ran in this family.

"Welcome to South Carolina and the Royall madhouse," Tammy said. Nate decided that Tammy, with her bubbly personality, could have played a starring role in one of those 60's beach movies.

"I'm happy to meet y'all." He smiled at Missy. "I can certainly see where Lauren gets her good looks." He handed Missy the gift he'd brought, a gourmet pack of BBQ sauce. "I know you folks are proud of your barbeque in this neck of the woods, but thought you might enjoy a little Texas flavor."

Missy peeked inside the gift bag, then wrapped her arm through his. "Sam loves to experiment, so I'm sure he'll put this to good use. I have refreshments out back. Let's get acquainted."

Nate reached back, grabbed Lauren's hand and tugged until she was snug against his side. He slipped an arm around her waist as Missy led them out on to a large wooden deck. He paused a moment absorbing the place where Lauren grew up. Lush landscaping encircled a large expanse of lawn. Massive live oak trees offered shade. A children's' swing and playhouse occupied one corner and a large shed the other. Adjacent homes hid behind tall shrubs. A light breeze off the ocean relieved the oppressive heat and humidity.

Steering Lauren toward a free-standing, two-seater swing, he guided her onto the wooden bench. "I'll get our snacks. What would you like?"

She started to rise, and he put a hand on her shoulder. "No, please, let me serve you for a change."

Her smile waivered with emotion. "Okay."

He hated to see her usual fire and passion relegated to some far corner. He sighed, remembering the way he'd gone through the motions in the early weeks after Sharon's death. As much as possible, he'd surrounded himself with the familiar. That way he didn't have to think, just do, and doing—putting one foot in front of the other each day—had given him time to adjust. The thing he hadn't done was feel the grief. Instead he'd pushed it away. He would do what he could over the next week to encourage her to talk, accept her silence when that's what she needed, hold her when she cried—something he should have allowed himself to do— and simply be with her.

Nate stood at the table next to Missy and perused the assortment of finger sandwiches, salads, and desserts. "You folks sure know how to throw a little something together. Does Lauren have any favorites in this spread?"

"Try the egg salad, and the turkey and cranberry sandwiches." She leaned in conspiratorially. "Between you and me, her secret vice is Hummingbird Cake." Missy pointed to a multi-layer cake thickly frosted with some rich cream concoction.

"Really? She always eats so healthy when she's with me. Makes me eat that green stuff."

Missy chuckled. "We all have our secrets." She poured

several glasses of sweetened tea and distributed them to waiting hands.

Nate sat down on the swing next to Lauren, causing it to gently rock. Missy took a chair next to Lauren, and Sam took a chair next to Nate. Tammy and Adam placed a small table in front of the swing and pulled up chairs, forming a semi-circle around their sister. He admired the well-oiled machine that was the Royall family, and the way they blanketed Lauren in a protective cloak. Reminded him a lot of his family. He hadn't understood until months later, how much his family had softened the blow. Without them, he wouldn't have made it.

Missy began the salvo. "Is this your first trip to South Carolina?"

"Yes, ma'am, between school and setting up my practice, I haven't strayed much beyond Texas. A situation I plan to remedy moving forward. A wise person," he patted Lauren's knee, "once told me new experiences help a person grow."

"Well then, Lauren will have to show you around." Missy took a dainty bite of her sandwich.

Sam's pleasing tenor entered the conversation. "I built that swing you're sitting on and am working on a matching high-back bench. Want to come to my workshop and see it?"

Nate got the hidden message. Sam wanted to talk to him in private—father to some guy interested in his daughter at a time when she needed to be sheltered. "Love to. My brothers and I just finished a gazebo for the backyard."

"Don't give my lovely wife any ideas." Sam bent and kissed Missy on the cheek.

The two men strolled across the yard to the large shed. Sam opened the double doors and Nate followed him inside. Huge windows on two walls and skylights overhead let in lots of natural light. He was pretty sure his mouth was hanging open and his eyes were bugging out, but he couldn't help himself. Every woodworking tool a person could imagine either hung on the wall or took up space as a free-standing unit. A large screen television was mounted high on the wall in one corner.

"Wow," Nate said as he slowly circled the space examining the various tools and equipment. "This is an impressive set up. Good thing you don't live closer to San Antonio or I'd be on your doorstep constantly." His fingers itched to pick them up and feel the heft of them in his hands.

Sam chuckled. "You'd have to get in line with my son and son-in-law. I started building things as a boy and it stuck with me. My projects keep me grounded."

Nate squatted down to take a closer look at a beautiful hope chest. "You're quite a craftsman." His hand reverently skimmed over the polished surface. "Not that I can match your skill, but I wish I had more time to do things like this."

"Speaking of time, South Carolina's a long way to come, especially when you have a busy veterinary practice. Am I correct in assuming you have more than a casual interest in my daughter?"

Nate rose slowly, his gut clenching. He let out a slow breath doing his best to relax into the rightness of what he felt for Lauren. "I do, sir. She's an amazing woman. I know she's hurting, and I want to provide whatever ease and comfort I can."

"I'm glad to hear that. My daughter's in a fragile place right now and doesn't need anyone to add to her troubles." Sam crossed his arms against his chest.

Nate respected the determination and protectiveness he saw in the other man's eyes. "Lauren means more to me than any other woman ever has. I have no intention of adding to her pain. I lost someone I cared about. I know what she's going through and only want to help her heal."

Sam clapped a hand on Nate's shoulder, his hand remaining a few seconds longer than necessary. "I'm glad we understand each other. You seem like a good man, and I'm trusting you to do right by my daughter. Let's go back and join the others."

****

191

Over the course of the whirlwind week, Nate figured they'd seen every site there was to see within a 50 mile radius. They'd driven up to Myrtle Beach one day, spent another touring plantations, and on another taken a boat out to Fort Sumter. Nate felt intense gratitude for the brief periods when grief slowly eased out of Lauren's eyes and the old Lauren reemerged. His heart ached when he listened to her wonder if she might have missed something and been responsible for her client's death. He was sure she hadn't, but self-recrimination was part of the process.

He'd also gotten to know Lauren's family—even met Ben and Daphne who Skyped in from Los Angeles. In the last six days, they'd talked, they'd laughed, they'd hugged and kissed, and in Nate's mind, they'd moved into official coupledom. She wasn't in the same place yet and it hurt when she pulled back. He understood her desire to keep her emotions on an even keel, especially the desire to avoid the potential for heartbreak. He'd done the same, only worse.

Today they were touring Charleston. He could see why people fell in love with the place. It was like stepping back in time a couple hundred years. Stately antebellum mansions, oak trees draped in Spanish moss, streets lined with charming row houses, the Historic City Market filled with artisans, even the traffic moved at a leisurely pace compared to San Antonio.

A late afternoon downpour caught them without umbrellas. They jogged back to his car like a couple of care-free teenagers and hightailed it over the bridge to Mt. Pleasant and his hotel. He hadn't experienced this sense of lightness, like he was floating on water, in years. He'd been right to come and stupid to have ever pushed her away. Moments like this, when he could give her the gift of stepping outside her grief, chased the fear of loving again back into the dungeon where it belonged.

He parked in the lot. Together they made a mad dash for the lobby and charged up the stairs to his third floor room. The room door crashed open, then closed with a thud. Lips and hands seemed everywhere at once as he pressed Lauren up against the wall. Soggy clothes hit the floor and they staggered toward the bed.

The bed bounced as their bodies flopped, laughing and playful. He buried his hands in her silken hair, breathed in the scent of rain and fresh air on her skin and locked their lips in a long, mind-drugging kiss. He rolled her on top of him so his hands and mouth could feast on the swell of her breasts. There was nothing more erotic than the feel of her nipple against his tongue as he laved it into a tight bud. He heard her velvety hum of pleasure and legs brushing against sheets. A delicious heat radiated from his groin, up his chest, and on into his brain shutting down all thought except for this exquisite creature in his arms. Her soft thighs straddling him created an inferno of desire signaling urgent messages to his erection to seek the warm, moist home waiting for it. The scent of sex surrounded them.

His finger found her feminine nub and circled until her hands gripped his shoulders like a vice and she rocked against him. His hands grasped her hips and guided her over his manhood. Her moan of delight nearly sent him over the edge but he held back, waiting for her to reach the pinnacle. Together they jumped off the cliff, experienced the heart-pounding drop, the jerk of the parachute opening, the slow floating, and the soft landing in a meadow filled with tall grass and wildflowers.

After they'd recuperated wrapped in each other's arms, he'd gotten up and taken their wet clothes to the hotel laundry room. Now they sat on the bed propped amongst pillows, sipping hot tea from the room coffee maker, making small talk. Sharing those little things that couples share. She was dressed in one of his t-shirts and he, only in a pair of sweat pants. He liked the way her fingers trailed up and down his arm as they talked.

"Next week I'm having lunch with Ashley's mother, hoping I can talk her into coming to the wedding. Not looking forward to that visit," Lauren said, "but even though

Ashley says she doesn't care, I know she does. I'd do anything to make Ashley's burden a little lighter."

"Are you sure you're up to it? Zach told me Mrs. Drayton is a… handful." Lauren's laughter told him, his expression gave away what he'd really been thinking.

She sighed. "Probably not, but I'll feel better about myself knowing I tried."

He leaned over and gently captured her earlobe between his lips hoping to win one of her achingly beautiful smiles. His body felt joyful as a beach ball bobbing on the waves when the corner of her mouth quirked up. "I admire what you're trying to do. I hear it takes a lot of guts to face a dragon."

"Speaking of facing dragons or demons," her voice softened. "Experiencing my client's death helped me understand, in a very small way, what you went through. While it was nothing like losing a fiancé, it shook my world." She stroked a hand down his cheek.

He snagged her hand and kissed her palm. He loved that even in pain, her first instinct was to comfort others.

"I understand why you needed time to heal and needed to protect yourself from more of life's sucker punches," she said. "Living creatures are designed to shy away from pain. It made sense on an intellectual level, but now I get it on a personal level." She lightly rubbed her head against his shoulder like the family pet seeking to be close to the one it loves. "I told you about my friend in high school who committed suicide?"

He nodded. Felt her tension.

"What I never said was that I felt guilty because I didn't think I'd done enough to help her."

Her tears dampened his chest where her cheek rested. "I know. The one time you talked about her, I sensed your pain and suspected you carried the burden of blame."

"I thought I'd confronted all of that in grad school during my training. Todd's death made me realize I hadn't. I think I'm finally on the path to forgiving myself."

He cupped her chin, angling her face toward him, and kissed her lightly on the lips, hoping she could feel how committed he was to her. "I never would have faced my grief, let it in without counseling. It was the best thing I ever did." He put an arm around her shoulders and snuggled her closer. "Until I could address what I was really afraid of, I was stuck in place. I'm glad you're finding your way free." He stroked her hair fascinated by the silky strands beneath his palm.

"Jasmine helped me understand the role my grandparents' death played in how I reacted to Sharon's death. So much in our lives is interconnected." His voice filled with emotion and fell to a hoarse whisper. "I've finally learned to let it go at least as much as any of us can." Her weight as she leaned into him heralded what life could be. "You were a big part of that. Talking to you about Sharon finally opened the floodgates and gave me the push I needed to embrace my grief. Opened the way for a second chance."

Lauren turned his head urging him to look into her eyes. A request he happily accepted. "I'm glad counseling helped and that talking to me made a difference. It's not easy to look into our dark places, face them for what they are, and make a conscious decision to live our lives differently. I'm proud of you."

He traced her lips with his fingertip. "Thank you for being there for me."

She traced the outline of his fingers against the sheet. "The last few weeks have been a journey of self-exploration for me as well. Between questioning whether or not I'm cut out to counsel other people and feeling like a big lump of unformed clay, I've learned a few important lessons. One, I know I am a healer. That's who I am, and painful as it might be at times, I can't run from who I am. Two, that big lump of clay that is me, it's waiting to be shaped into something I can't even imagine right now. A better version of me."

Pulling her across his body so he could cradle her in his arms, he kissed her eyelids, trailed kisses from her temple down to her lips. She was already one of the kindest, most caring people he knew. He couldn't wait to see the butterfly that would emerge. She twisted to fling a leg across his. Her breasts nestled against his chest and her feminine core teased his manhood. Turns out he was ready to play again.

As the glow of their latest lovemaking session slid into contentment, he glanced at his watch. "Our clothes should be dry by now." He levered himself off the bed and slipped on a t-shirt and flip flops. "I'll be right back. We need to be at your folks in an hour. Much as I'd like to stay here, we'd better get moving.

Walking down the hall, Nate knew for sure he wanted Lauren to be his wife. Tomorrow morning he'd return to San Antonio, taking with him what Sam had shared privately after dinner last night. 'Son,' he'd said, 'if you and Lauren ever decide to make your relationship permanent, we'd be thrilled to welcome you to our family.'

Now wasn't the right time to ask. One more hurdle to overcome. She needed more healing time, but as soon as she was ready, he'd be down on bended knee, heart in his hand.

CHAPTER TWENTY FIVE

Before she reached Ashley's front door, Lauren heard her dogs whining and their nails clacking against the tile floor. She'd stopped at home long enough to drop her bags and then made a beeline to pick up her dogs. Holding them by their collars, Ashely did her best to restrain them, but her petite frame fought a losing battle. Lauren stepped inside and slammed the door. A ball of black fluff scampered to Lauren's feet, squatted, and peed.

"Sorry, we're still working on bladder control." Ashley dropped the towel she'd wedged under her arm over the puddle and mashed it with her foot. Releasing the dogs she embraced her pal while the dogs clamored for attention.

Lauren knelt down, but swiftly ended up on her back engulfed in fur and wagging tails, their tongues making short work of her makeup. With a final hug, she shoved the dogs away and stood up. Home. The time away had been good for her, but she was ready to get back to her life. She didn't plan to jump back in like she once would have, but instead ease her way down the steps and into the water slowly. Giving herself time to adjust to the change in temperature. She'd learned moderation in life was a good thing. She'd also learned this was where she wanted to be—probably for the rest of her life.

Bending, Lauren scooped up the ball of fur. "Where did this little…" She held the puppy at arm's length peering at its belly, "princess, come from?"

"Zach said I needed a dog to be a proper ranch wife." Ashley took the little black Lab from Lauren and cradled it against her chest. "Between you and me, I think he saw Matt's litter and visions of hunting trips started dancing in his head." Ashley led the way to the kitchen.

She opened the patio door and shooed the two big dogs out, before putting the puppy down. It scampered after its idols. "If that man thinks he's getting me in a duck blind at the crack of dawn..." She pursed her lips and shook her head. "*So not happening.*"

"I'm fairly confident, his hunting agenda leans more toward getting together with the guys, drinking beer, shooting guns, and being all macho," Lauren did a decent imitation of a body building pose, "not spending time with his lady love." A lingering sadness continued to shadow her steps, but it wasn't oppressive like being locked in a damp cave anymore. After a month, there were more light days than dark, though she never knew when a cloudburst would hit. She was ready to start living her life again.

Ashley's tinkling laugh swirled around the kitchen. "Tea's already brewed and on the table. Plop your butt in the chair, grab a pen, and start addressing envelopes."

Lauren eyed the two, tall stacks of creamy, linen envelopes. "Good Lord. Is everyone in Texas getting an invitation?"

"No, only half." Ashley slid into a chair and held up her hands. "Gloria June has another huge stack. If I'd known I'd have this many invitations to address, I might not have been so quick to agree to a December wedding." Ashley poured tea into two china cups. "Luckily, my family isn't nearly as extensive or we'd be here forever."

Lauren picked up a pen and removed the top sheet of addresses from the pile. "Speaking of family... I had lunch with your mother last week, and you owe me big time. Unfortunately, nothing's changed." One of those cloudbursts drifted back into Lauren's sphere and she felt the pressure of tears behind her eyelids. She closed her eyes, breathed slowly, and used her meditation techniques until the feeling passed.

Ashley put her hand over Lauren's. "Thank you for

trying. How are you doing?"

"Accepting there will be good days and bad. Grateful that the experience gave me the opportunity to reevaluate my approach to my clients. Going forward, more listening, greater empathy, and less certainty that I know exactly what they need without a good deal more reflection." She picked up her pen and fingered the pile of envelopes. "I'm sorry I couldn't do more about your mother."

"I didn't figure she'd change her mind. My father doesn't care one way or the other as long as it doesn't interfere with business. Thank you for trying. I can rest easy knowing I've done everything I can to encourage them to be part of their only daughter's wedding."

Sadness wove its way through Ashley's voice and into Lauren's heart. The impulse to wade in and make everything better, slammed into her. She wished there was something she could do, but if the last month had taught her nothing else, she'd learned—and accepted—there were some things she couldn't fix.

"There's a bright side to everything." Lauren reached over and patted her friend's hand. "Despite your mother's best efforts, you turned into an amazing woman and," she held up a finger, "Your mother's going to miss the best dang party north of the Rio Grande." The two high-fived.

"Damn straight she is," Ashley said.

Lauren slid another envelop in front of her. She paused, put the pen down and braced her forearms on the table. "In the long run, I think they'll regret their decision. Your wedding is one moment in time and they can never get it back." Brushing a tear from her eye, her throat clogged with emotion. Ashley was strong, but Lauren couldn't help wishing a life filled with rainbows and sunshine for her friend.

"I agree." Ashley swiped a stray tear from her cheek and took a deep breath. "I can't change who they are. Mother told me if I insisted on marrying beneath me—in a barn, no less—they couldn't be part of it." Ashley picked up her cup, her hand shaking. She sipped and placed the cup back on its saucer, determination creating fine lines around her eyes. "My wedding day will be filled with love and laughter, not judgement and condescension. Bad attitudes can darn well stay home." Her tiny fist struck the table.

"Screw anyone who isn't happy on your big day." Lauren's laughter rose from her belly up. "Whenever I feel down, you always cheer me up." She realized while her life had changed forever with Todd's death, dealing with the good and bad that life throws our way, provides opportunities for growth. It's up to us to grab those opportunities with both hands and learn from them. She planned to use what she'd learned to be a better therapist and a better person. She wished with all her heart Nate was destined to be part of her life, but understood now the struggles he'd had reaching for the love he wanted. Loving could bring great joy, but it also could bring great pain. Was he at the point where he was willing to take the risk?

****

Lauren adored summer in the Texas Hill Country. The air shimmered with heat, the sky a blue arc above. Driving out to Nate's ranch, windows down, her hair lifting in the breeze flowing through the car was like a balm to her soul. Her dogs in the back seat, pushed their noses through the opening, ears fluttering like flags, savoring the chance to breathe in new smells. Life, or as she liked to think of it, her post-Todd life, was slowly returning to normal. Different now, but in many ways, better.

Nate's attentiveness since her return, kept a permanent smile on her face. The weeks had stretched into a month. They'd had so much fun, truly enjoying every chance they had to be together. She was his fan girl and understood now why women squealed when they spotted their favorite star. Anticipation and hope fluttered in her belly like an army of butterflies whenever Nate was near—and even when he wasn't. She was in love. She recognized the signs, accepted them. Heck, she embraced them and was willing to wait as long as it took for Nate to love her back. He hadn't said anything about making their relationship permanent, but his recent thoughtfulness spoke silently of promises yet to be made.

His clinic, which fronted the highway, came into view. She passed it and turned into the next long, graveled drive. Soon his house loomed large, begging to be filled with the laughter of children. A rope swing would hang from the massive oak over there. A playhouse would nestle under its leafy umbrella—little girls in princess dresses serving tea to little boys playing pirate. Nate's strides would shorten to let tiny ones keep up with him as he went about his chores. He'd be great with children, a wonderful father. She braked in his driveway. Don't get ahead of yourself a warning nagged her subconscious.

He stepped out of the barn. Her breath caught at the sight of him. Dressed in jeans that caressed his thighs, a black t-shirt that flowed over a chest and biceps as big as Texas. Prowling toward her like a lion, she sighed. Hard not to let her dreams get ahead of reality.

She parked in the shade of a tree. As soon as she was out of the car strong arms snaked around her, sandwiching her between the car door and his hard length. His mobile lips captured hers in a knee-buckling kiss. She opened her mouth granting access to his roguish tongue, her body humming with desire. She inhaled his scent of country life and virile male. The passenger door bumped her hip. Without breaking the kiss he'd somehow managed to let the dogs out. He eased back, framing her face in his hands, gazing intently into her eyes.

"I've missed you." His forehead rested against hers and his fingers tunneled into her hair. "It's only been two days, but it feels like years since I last touched you."

"I know. I feel the same way." She tilted her lips until they touched his.

"Did you pack the picnic lunch?" he asked.

"It's in the back and includes fried chicken and cornbread as requested."

Keeping her hand in his, he walked around the car, lifted the rear hatch and removed the wicker picnic basket. He reached for the glass baking dish beside the basket.

"No leave that one. It's dessert." She put her hand on his. "I thought it might be nice to eat that later on the back patio. Afterwards…" She raised her brows suggesting intimacy was part of the plan.

"Didn't I hear it's best to start with dessert in case the world ends before you get to it?"

"I think we're safe. Trail ride and picnic first. Dessert later." Though if he pressed the issue, she could be persuaded.

"Woman, you drive a hard bargain." He brought her hand to his mouth and nibbled the soft skin of her palm before leading her toward the stable.

"I'll transfer this to the saddle bags and we can be on our way." He paused opening the plastic container inhaling the spicy aroma of the chicken. "Smells like a touch of chili pepper."

"If you can smell the pepper, maybe I put too much in. We better not eat it." She reached for the container, but he quickly stowed it in the saddlebag.

"Smells perfect to me." He grabbed the reins of both horses and led them outside. They both mounted and set off on the trail.

She relaxed into the rhythm of the horse as they rode along a meadow dotted with red oak and maples. Cattle grazed creating a serene tableau.

"I thought we'd picnic along the creek. There's a nice spot up ahead."

They arrived at a grassy clearing that extended to the creek bank. Nate dismounted and laid a blanket under a tree. "This is one of my favorite spots. The calm pours into me whenever I'm here."

"I can see why." She took his hand and stood by his side gazing across the tranquil landscape. She'd never felt so at one with another human being. Moving slowly, not wanting to disturb the mood, she set the food out on the blanket. They enjoyed quiet conversation, basked in the sunshine filtering through the trees, listened to the rustling of the leaves, and the rippling of water over stones while they ate. Then Nate broke the silence and the peace.

"I wanted to be somewhere quiet to talk. My thinking place seemed fitting."

"Talk about what?" A stab of fear, sharp like a paper cut, shot through her. They were in such a good space right now. She didn't want to disturb the growing closeness that had developed over the past few weeks. She set her half-finished plate of food on the blanket. Hunger fleeing her clenching stomach.

"You. Me." He picked up her hand and toyed with her fingers, kicking her heart rate up a notch. "I want you to know how important you are to me. I want you to know I'm here for you—always will be." He tangled his fingers in her hair. "I told you in South Carolina I can see my way forward now." Leaning in, his lips brushed hers. "I want you to know, I'm finally feeling good about myself and my future."

"You've been changing for months, less wary, more open. Good changes. Solid changes." She hoped she would be a part of that future he envisioned—a big part. So far, he hadn't said anything. Time to nudge him? "I, for one, am looking forward to seeing what the future holds for you. Any thoughts on the matter?"

"A few." He stood up and offered her his hand. "Time to get back to the house. I hear dessert calling."

His mischievous grin sent sparks of excitement up her spine. The man had more than Pineapple Upside Down cake on his mind. Fine with her, since his train of thought meshed so perfectly with her own.

****

That evening, sitting on a lounge chair on the patio, she snuggled into the light shawl around her shoulders. Replete and languid after the hot sex they'd shared followed by a dinner of hearty vegetable beef soup and homemade biscuits, life was grand. What else could a woman ask for? A little voice whispered, staying right here. Like this. Forever.

Nate squatted in front of the outdoor fireplace, throwing a few more logs on the fire. She wasn't convinced she needed the extra heat the way his jeans molded his firm behind, but a fire was a nice touch. So were the candles in hurricane lanterns he'd placed here and there. Frank Sinatra's voice crooned softly in the background and the fresh flowers in a vase on the table were a nice touch.

Apparently the man wanted to set the mood. For what? They'd already made love, so seduction seemed unlikely. She shrugged, too content to ponder his motives. The lounge dipped under his weight as he sat on the edge and faced her. She moved her legs to make room for him.

"You asked this afternoon if I had any thoughts about my future. I didn't answer then, but I'd like to now." He'd lightly grasped her upper arms and she felt his hands tremble.

She placed a hand on his thigh. "What's wrong?"

"Nothing's wrong. At least I don't think anything's wrong. In fact, I'm hoping everything is…" He ran his hands through his hair. "I am making such a mess of this. I write poetry. You'd think I'd be good with words." He took a deep breath and sat up straighter, gathering her hands in both of his and resting them on his knees.

"Nate, you're scaring me." Dread beat like a bass drum through her blood.

"No. No, honey. Don't be scared." He pressed her hands to his heart. "Feel that?"

She nodded. Uncertainty ruled, but possibility scrabbled for a tenuous toehold.

"That's my heart beating for you. When you left for South Carolina, one of my wiseass brothers asked, 'Could I live without you?' I realized, the answer is no. You're the air I breathe. You make the dark places light. I want you by my side every day and every night. I want you to be the mother of my children. I've never wanted anything like I want you."

He slid off the chair and down on one knee. She thought for sure her heart would burst it was so full.

"Thank you for not giving up on me—even when I'd given up on myself—for helping me see what was missing in my life and giving me the courage to go after it." He pulled a small, velvet box out of his pocket and opened it. A breathtaking, pillow-cut center diamond, surrounded by smaller diamonds, mounted on a band with intricate scroll work winked back at her. 'Please marry me?"

"Oh, my goodness. Oh, my goodness." She might not be able to breathe, but she could leap. The lounge tipped to its side as she launched herself into his arms, knocking him on that fabulous butt of his. Fisting his hair in her hands, she locked her lips on his.

He cupped her shoulders, pushing her back, giving them both a moment to catch their breath. "Is that a yes?"

She nodded. "Yes." Tears streamed down her cheeks.

"Then let's make this official." He slipped the ring from the box, and holding her left hand, guided the ring onto her finger. Strong arms wrapped around her and they sealed their love with a kiss.

CHAPTER TWENTY SIX

The hairdresser added a final pin to keep Ashley's veil in place. The photographer hovered like a hummingbird, flitting around and snapping away. The florist inserted the bouquets into pretty, crystal vases, then scurried off with the box of boutonnieres and corsages to distribute them. The wedding planner had already swooped in and out, ensuring everything was on schedule. The temperature was mild for December but they still didn't want to keep their guests waiting for long.

Outside, the caterer set up the last row of chairs in front of the flower-decked gazebo. Next they would move to the barn to set up for the reception. The string quartet had arrived and was tuning its instruments. Lauren peeked out the lace-covered window in time to see the Pastor get out of his car. Long strides took him to the porch of Zach's house where the men had congregated. Soft music filtered into the room as the ushers began seating the first guests. Happy energy swirled around them like a mini tornado.

"It's really happening." Ashley and Crystal joined Lauren at the window. "My wedding day." The quiet click of the camera continued in the background.

"Happy?" Lauren asked, hugging her friend, careful to avoid mussing the soft tulle skirt of Ashley's ballroom gown.

"Ecstatic. Nervous. Emotional. A little sad."

"Your parents?" Crystal asked.

Ashley nodded, exhaling a long breath. "Yes, I'm sad about their decision," she accepted the antique hanky Lauren pressed into her hand, "but when I had to choose between them and Zach—no contest. It's Zach all the way. No question. No hesitation."

"Can I get you three by the four-poster bed?" The photographer motioned them to stand at the foot of the bed. "Ashley, you in the middle. Put your arms around each other. Perfect. Now one with your bouquets." Her assistant handed them the flowers.

"Let's get one over by the armoire. Lauren and Crystal, kneel down and arrange Ashley's train. Wonderful." A gentle tap sounded at the door and Gloria June stepped in along with the wedding planner.

Gloria June gasped softly and her hand covered her mouth. "You're breathtaking. Like a fairytale princess." She used her own antique hanky to dab at her eyes. "I won't be a moment, but I wanted to give you this before the wedding." She held out a vintage necklace of intricate daisies encrusted with seed-pearls and diamonds.

Slowly stretching out her hand, Ashley fingered the delicate piece. "I'm speechless."

"It first belonged to my grandmother, then my mother, then me, and now you."

Ashley removed the pearls she was wearing. "It would mean a lot to me if I could wear your gift for the wedding. Would you mind helping me with it?"

Gloria June moved behind Ashely and fastened the clasp. The center daisy rested just below the hollow of her throat. Ashley moved to the mirror, surrounded by her soon to be mother-in-law and two bridesmaids. With a feather-light touch, Ashely stroked the dainty piece.

Whirling quickly, Ashley threw her arms around Gloria June's neck, hugging her tightly. "I can't wait to join your family."

"You already are part of the family, but we can't wait to make it official." Gloria June swiveled and pulled Lauren over so she could hug both women to her side. "Just think, in May, I get to welcome my second daughter into the fold." She looked from Ashley to Lauren. "I don't know how I managed to win the daughter-in-law lottery, but I'm not complaining."

The wedding planner coughed discretely. "Mrs. Kincaid, you need to join your husband in the staging area... and ladies, it's time to make our way downstairs. Ceremony starts in ten minutes."

Gloria June slipped into the hallway after one last glance. They helped each other into the ballet shrugs Lauren had knit and opened the door.

****

Lauren thought she was prepared to see Nate standing next to his brother on the steps of the gazebo. After all, yesterday afternoon at the rehearsal she'd only felt the normal kick of excitement as she boogied down the aisle to Party for Two by Shania Twain. It had been all light-hearted fun and giggles.

Today was different. Maybe it was the tuxedo that made Nate look like something out of a romantic movie. Maybe it was the moving strains of the string quartet playing Canon in D by Pachelbel. Maybe it was the smiling guests dressed in their finest eager to catch a glimpse of the bride. Most likely, when her eyes locked on Nate's, it was the realization that in a few short months she would be the woman walking toward her soul mate, her future, her dreams. Swallowing past the lump in her throat, Lauren moved to her place on the gazebo steps.

The ceremony flew by. Vows recited—Ashley's voice a clear, calm soprano while Zach's tenor waivered with controlled emotion. Rings exchanged. The bride and groom kissed. After that, nothing but impressions.

Lots of hand shaking and back slapping in the old fashioned receiving line. Guests wandered into one of the small barns for socializing, appetizers, and liquid libations. Pictures, pictures, and more pictures. Whenever he could get close enough, Nate's warm hand was on her back and lips on whatever part of her body was exposed and socially acceptable. Someone shoved a plate of food in her hand. She hadn't eaten much before the ceremony and was ravenous. Sharing a spring roll with Nate, lips meeting in the middle. Whisked off to bustle the bride's train. Seated at the head table with the rest of the wedding party. Smiling constantly. Making a toast. She vaguely remembered a meal being in there somewhere. Watching Ashley and Zach cut the cake. First dance.

Finally, with most of the expected wedding activities out of the way, the band blasted everyone on to the dance floor. This part of the evening didn't have to end as far as she was concerned. Granted, there were the obligatory dances with her brothers and Ashley's brothers, her father and Zach's father, but most of the evening she luxuriated in the feel of Nate's arms around her.

"Okay, ladies and gents, we have a special surprise for y'all," the band leader announced.

She did a double-take as Nate, Zach, and Josh headed for the stage. They picked up their guitars and strummed a few practice chords. Zach stepped up to the microphone.

"This song is dedicated to Ashley Kincaid. My wife." His grin stretched almost ear-to-ear. "I can hardly belief my good fortune—Ashley, my wife. I like the sound of that." He blew a kiss out to her and the guests cheered. "I wrote the tune and Nate wrote the lyrics. Here goes…"

Their voices wove through the song, creating a tapestry of longing, devotion, and a total sense of completion. Soul mates who found each other despite all odds.

The last notes vibrated out into the night, reaching for the stars. With tears streaming down her face, Lauren heard Gloria June stage-whisper to Jack, "Well, father, we have two of our boys settled with good women. One more to go."

"Hush, now," Jack said, but kissed his wife on the forehead. "Give the boy a chance. His divorce will only be final next month."

"I know, but Josh deserves the same happiness his brothers have found. A mama can only hope."

Yes, she wished with all her fix-everyone's-problems heart that Josh would find his happy ending. She'd gotten to know him well during their counseling sessions. He was a good man.

When Nate left the stage, he marched straight to her, swept her into his arms, and twirled her around, everything and everyone faded into the background. Her life was joy and love in abundance.

- THE END -

If you enjoyed My Sexy Veterinarian, I'd love to hear about it. Honest reviews on Amazon, Barnes & Noble, Goodreads, or other review sites are always appreciated.

OTHER BOOKS

Julia's Star
My Rodeo Man: The Texas Kincaids #1

Please visit my website at
www.bonniephelpsauthor.com
to learn more about me and my books.

ABOUT THE AUTHOR

Rumor has it that Bonnie began telling stories at a very early age. Photos exist of the author toddling around the corner of the house covered in mud babbling about magic rabbits leading her through the garden. Her parents were amused only adding fuel to the fire of her passion for writing. From then on, her active imagination continued to churn out plots and character sketches always wondering how different people would behave in similar situations. People are endlessly fascinating and stories are everywhere. She loves exploring, rearranging and weaving her narratives throughout her characters' lives.

When she is not mucking around in her own characters' lives, you will find her perusing her Kindle and reading someone else's story. She also enjoys baking, taking long walks and people watching. Bonnie writes Contemporary Romance and lives in Northern California with her husband.

Have a question or comment? Send Bonnie an email at: bonnie@bonniephelpsauthor.com

Made in the USA
San Bernardino, CA
07 July 2017